NOBODY'S DOG

NOBODY'S DOG

by Ria Voros

Scholastic Canada Ltd.

Toronto New York London Auckland Sydney
Mexico City New Delhi Hong Kong Buenos Aires

Scholastic Canada Ltd.
604 King Street West, Toronto, Ontario M5V 1E1, Canada

Scholastic Inc.
557 Broadway, New York, NY 10012, USA

Scholastic Australia Pty Limited
PO Box 579, Gosford, NSW 2250, Australia

Scholastic New Zealand Limited
Private Bag 94407, Botany, Manukau 2163, New Zealand

Scholastic Children's Books
Euston House, 24 Eversholt Street, London NW1 1DB, UK

Library and Archives Canada Cataloguing in Publication
Voros, Ria
Nobody's dog / by Ria Voros.

ISBN 978-1-4431-1913-9

I. Title.

PS8643.O76N62 2012 jC813'.6 C2012-901672-1

Cover photograph: Laura Stanley
Author photograph: Théodora Armstrong

6 5 4 3 2 1 Printed in Canada 121 12 13 14 15 16

For Pender, whose pawprints are all over this story, both in the lessons he taught me and the love I was privileged to give him.

— R. V.

CHAPTER 1

The car turns over three times. Hits the curb, goes up on its side like a stunt in a movie. Rolls down the bank, crashing through trees and bushes that break windows and scratch the doors and roof. It's loud and close, happening in my brain, not outside it, but then we stop, upside down, and everything gets quiet. Something creaks, drips. A small motor whirrs on and on, like it forgot to break. I think, That was fast. *It's hard to breathe — the seat belt holds me tight. I think,* What? What was fast? *Someone groans in the front seat. Mom. Dad. I think about speaking. Drip, drip, whirr. I forget what I was going to say.*

It flies right over my head. Up there in the bright blue sky, the final evidence that I'm alone. This is the last time I'll see my only friend, and I can't even see him — only the white airplane I imagine him sitting in, probably eating peanuts and watching the city disappear below. I stare at the white puffy trail until it blurs and fades and the plane is gone behind the mountains. My neck hurts from looking up so long.

Around me, guys yell at each other, play scrappy basketball, girls giggle in groups like it's a normal day in their normal lives. I guess it is. School just let out on the fourth last day before summer break. Everyone's got plans to brag about, classes to skip. This year, my first year of high school, started all right because I at least had a friend to hang out with. But then there was the accident. Everything stopped. For a while, that included my brain. I had to go to a psychologist, Dr. Tang, twice a week so he could tell me how broken I was and how I could get fixed. I didn't make a lot of progress with him. Or with anything else. You could say I checked out for a while, and I got excused from a lot of stuff. *Don't worry, Jakob. We understand, under the circumstances*, teachers would tell me. *Just do what you can*. Or as my dad used to say when he drove us home on rainy winter nights after a movie, *Just keep it between the ditches*.

I take the short route, straight past the playing fields and park. I picture Grant in his airplane seat, writing a play-by-play of the journey for me, which he'll send as soon as he gets to London. His family's moving there for two years and he only found out about it a few months ago. We didn't have much time to say goodbye or do all the things we'd planned for this summer. We crammed things into weekends and after school, but I still felt like there were hundreds of things we didn't get to do.

Grant and I became friends in September when we were in the same gym class. Neither of us could do more than ten push-ups. That was our first bonding moment. After Coach Slater shook his head sadly at me as he passed by with his clipboard, Grant slapped my shoulder and said, "Hey, me too. Want to form a perpetual disappointment club?" I'd had a few friends in elementary school, but somehow they'd moved on, found other kids to play with, and by grade seven, I was playing alone most of the time. I did my own thing, but it sucked to see them — my old so-called friends — hanging out with kids we'd always thought were jerks. So when Grant and I started hanging out and found we had stuff in common, things just got easier. We liked the same music and junk food. We started skateboarding together, though we were both terrible. We were going to try all these crazy stunts when we got the guts or when the summer came, whichever happened first.

My parents were always worried about me being a loner, but they hid it well. Not well enough, obviously. I could tell they were relieved that I was going to the park with Grant. They loved Grant. They wanted Grant to live with us. I couldn't imagine what they'd be like if I had ten friends.

But then everything changed. My parents and I were driving to the airport to go on Christmas vacation. Dark out. Wet, cold December streets. My dad and I were talking about something — then the memory goes to pieces and I wake up in the hospital with beeping machines and a really bad headache. Aunt Laura, my mom's sister, sent me to Dr. Tang, but I guess my brain was too messed up even for him. He tried a bunch of different things that were supposed to get me to remember — he said that was the only way I would be able to move on — but things stayed jumbled up and locked inside. Everyone kept expecting me to have clear memories of the accident, to suddenly know exactly what happened. All I got were separate, floating pieces of a puzzle, and a numb feeling, like my emotions were broken. In the end he told Aunt Laura it would take time. Then he gave her the bill and she hit the roof. She didn't send me back after that.

I didn't like thinking about it anyway. First I was a loner who finally had a friend, and then I was a loner with no parents and a hole in his memory. It felt easier if I imagined it happened to someone else. I didn't talk with Grant about it and he didn't ask. Actually, after the accident, when we hung out it was like letting air into a stuffy room. We'd skate or chill in the park or just surf the web and I'd get a break from the black hole in my memory. With Aunt Laura, everything is uncomfortable — neither of us wants to talk about it, or talk about not talking about it. Grant and I have our own language. He calls me J instead of Jakob. J's like my alter ego — me in a different world. He's braver and better at sports and talking back to adults. J doesn't care what others think. When Grant and I hang out, J's there. But when I'm not with Grant, the other me comes out, the me I've been from kindergarten — Jakob Nobody. My last name's Nebedy, so it was easy for kids to make that jump. "Hey, Nobody," they'd shout. "Nobody to play with? Nobody cares!"

When I get home from school, Aunt Laura's car isn't out front, which means she's working. Even though I can never keep her shifts straight, I know she's home if her car's there. She's an emergency room nurse, so she sees all the really screwed-up stuff right when it gets out of the ambulance, and gets home from her shifts exhausted and cranky. I'm not sure if this is what it's like for nurses in other parts of the hospital because she's been there for years. She even has a nickname for it — Emerg, which sounds like *emerge*, like it's something you come out of. Her friends come over once a month for a movie night and they all talk about how terrible their jobs are.

After the accident, Aunt Laura moved into our house. My house. Her house. It doesn't matter anymore. My parents left it to her, along with me, in their will. She'd always lived across town, but we didn't see her all the time. My mom never talked about it, but I knew there was something going on between them. I got the feeling Aunt Laura was jealous of my mom, like she'd never quite measured up when she and my mom were kids. It kind of made me glad I didn't have any siblings.

Last Thanksgiving I heard them talking in the living room. Aunt Laura was staying over because it was late and they were a little drunk. Dad had gone to bed and I sat with my door cracked and listened to them talk about guys they'd dated and places they had or hadn't travelled to. My mom was trying to convince Aunt Laura to move into the house. We had a suite downstairs that Dad had finished fixing up. He said that it was where they'd put me when they got tired of me leaving my dirty socks everywhere.

"I don't want to live under you," Aunt Laura said to my mom. "That's so — I don't know — shades of high school."

"Not at all," my mom said. "We had rooms at opposite ends of the house."

"Melissa, you know what I mean. I like where I live now."

"I know, but we're closer to the hospital. You could even bike to work. And you'd spend more time with Jakob. It's so important that you two are close."

Aunt Laura didn't reply.

I opened the door a little wider.

"Look, you'd be doing us a favour. Can you at least think about it?"

"You know, this is so typical," Aunt Laura said. There was an edge in her voice that made me want to stop listening, but I couldn't. Nothing could have made me move.

"Here we go again."

"No, you need to listen to me." Aunt Laura lowered her voice a little. "You've never had to pay for anything in your life. You got pregnant — Mom and Dad helped you. You had a shotgun wedding — Charlie's parents paid for it. I went into nursing because it was practical — such a smart choice according to everyone else — and I'm still in debt for it and I hate my job half the time. You wanted to study *poetry* for the love of it and you got the biggest scholarship in town."

"Don't be petty, Laura. And it wasn't that big a scholarship. This is ridiculous."

"No, it's not."

"What does it have to do with anything?"

"It's just part of the pattern."

"Right. The pattern." My mom didn't sound angry. She sounded tired. Like she'd heard all this before. I hadn't.

"You've had this charmed life that magically worked out while I struggled for everything, and I just don't think I should feel guilty if I don't want to save you. I don't want to live here. I have my own life."

My mom didn't say anything.

My heart drummed in my ears and I hoped it wasn't too loud to hear whatever they'd say next.

"I'm going to bed," my mom finally said. "Happy Thanksgiving, Laura."

"Melissa, don't be like that. I didn't mean it to sound harsh. I just — "

"How did you mean it, then? I can't help it if you feel hard done by. I didn't set out to have a better life than you. I don't think I do. I guess it's really about perspective. I see you as family and you see me as competition."

Aunt Laura didn't say anything for a moment. "I have

goals too, you know."

"And I guess they don't include being an aunt or a sister."

"Don't say that — you know I am."

My mom walked toward the hallway and I had to scramble back from my door. She spoke in a low voice, in a voice that said she was sad to be proved right. "Just not in the way I'd hoped you would be."

I walk over to the spot where Aunt Laura's car would be parked and across our scraggly front lawn that never grows, so it never needs mowing. If it did it would be my job, so I'm happy it's brown stubble. There are no lights on upstairs, but in the basement, where our tenant lives, a bedroom light shines yellow. Soleil moved in last month with her daughter, Libby. They're kind of odd, but Aunt Laura had interviewed so many awful people, she was just happy Soleil didn't have a drug problem and wasn't in a rock band.

We already know a lot about Soleil. She's kind of an open book — the kind that invites you to find out everything about her. She's been coming upstairs a lot recently, and Aunt Laura doesn't seem to mind. If I didn't know better I'd say my aunt might actually be getting along with someone outside the hospital. Soleil's an actor but she works at a pet groomer's while she looks for acting gigs. I've never seen anything she's been in, although she says she's done three commercials. Libby's twelve and completely different from her mom. She's skinny and bug-eyed and quiet. The kind of quiet that's weird — like the person's always watching you, seeing more than you want them to. Sometimes I catch her staring at me in a way that makes me feel like something under a microscope. She either thinks I'm scary or fascinating. I'm pretty sure she's embarrassed by her mom's crazy clothes. I guess I would be too — Soleil loves anything bright, short or tight. Libby always wears black and one other colour — each time I see her it's a bright green shirt or orange socks to her knees with black everything else. The other thing I know is Libby loves drawing. I find pieces of paper in the backyard or on the steps off the deck. I don't look at them because I don't want to encourage anything. I never know when she's watching me.

I let myself in the front door and go straight to my room. It's the only place in the house where I can relax and do what I want. If I hang out too much in the living room, Aunt Laura tells me to go outside, or worse, clean something up. But in my room, I have full reign. My walls are sky blue, like a day in July, and there are glow-in-the-dark stars on the ceiling that my dad put up years ago. He arranged them in actual constellations so I would know how to look for the real thing. Dad had an astronomy obsession. He told me once that he wished he'd stayed in science instead of doing math like his parents wanted him to. The stars don't really work anymore, but I'm too lazy to take them down. And I guess I'd feel weird. Plus, if any ceiling came off with the stars, I'd hear about it. Aunt Laura kind of took over when she moved in. Took out all my parents' stuff and wanted everything just like she had it at her old place. She painted all the rooms in the house. Except mine. She kind of acts like the house is hers now, after all that time of not wanting anything to do with it.

I throw my bag onto the bed and turn on my computer. It would be great if there was an email from Grant. He said if I paid him a hundred dollars he'd moon a flight attendant.

My email inbox is empty, so the next thing I check is

Dogzone. Nothing new since this morning. I go to Poochfinder. Two new entries. I lean back in the chair and click on the first link.

When I was five, I started asking my parents if I could get a dog. Any dog was fine, although since then I decided on some breeds. Big dogs — German shepherds, huskies and rottweilers. But they always said no. *Next year, maybe when you're older, maybe when you're in grade nine.* Since I've basically become an orphan, I've been pretty obsessed with getting a dog. Sometimes I get the feeling it's about more than that — like I'm trying to prove something to my parents. My dad just didn't get how important it was to me. I've been checking dog blogs, websites and forums for two years. Every day I check all the shelter websites for new dogs and imagine taking one of them home. A dog to be my buddy, always with me. Someone who'd never leave and wouldn't care if I did stupid things. I'm hoping if I can save up some money, I might be able to convince Aunt Laura to let me get one. Since she's not home a lot, it would keep me company. But first I have to find a job to make some money. If I show her how responsible I am, she can't use that as an excuse.

While I surf around, I crunch the last stale bites of a cracker left from yesterday. The phone rings beside me. For a second I think it's Grant.

"I'm going to be late," Aunt Laura says even before I say hello. "Make yourself some dinner, okay?"

This is nothing new. She's always *slaving away in Emerg,* as she says.

"No problem," I say. I'd rather be on my own anyway.

"Hey, didn't Grant leave today?"

"Yeah."

"I'm sorry, Jakob. I know you'll miss him."

I realize this might be a good time to score some sympathy for the dog situation. "Yeah, I really will. I was wondering, actually, if I could talk to you about dog adoptions again. I know you said no way last time, but I think I might have a better plan now."

"Jakob, we've been through this — "

"I know, but it's different this time."

"Jakob, I've got to go, okay? We're slammed here. We'll talk later, I promise." She hangs up before I can answer.

Today's Most Adoptable Dog:

Hi, I'm Laddy, a shepherd–lab cross. I'm four years old and still full of energy. My last home didn't have room for me, but if you take me home, I'll keep you entertained with lots of ball-chasing, running and as many tricks as you can teach me. **Note:** Laddy isn't good with small children and should go to a cat-free home.

Later, as I'm making myself Kraft Dinner in the microwave, Soleil knocks on the back door. Libby's there too — she says something to her mom I don't catch.

"Helloooo? Jakob?" Soleil presses her face to the window and her nose goes flat.

I let her in.

"Smells delish in here." Soleil steps inside in some kind of dressing gown with her hair all slicked back. It makes her look like a movie star waiting in her trailer. Libby follows, looking embarrassed. Her hair's in braids and she looks six years old.

I don't understand the two of them — one all dramatic and the other weird and quiet. I found one of Libby's drawings on the deck yesterday. I didn't move it or really look at it, but when I got home from school, it was folded up by our back door. I took it down the stairs to the suite and left it on their doormat.

"Whatcha got there?" Soleil peers into the microwave.

"Kraft Dinner, from scratch," I say.

"Yum. You should throw something else in there, make it more nutritious. Got any peas or carrots?" Soleil pokes around the kitchen. She knows how to make herself at home.

The microwave beeps and I pull out my bowl.

"Hey — you look down, J-man. Are you okay?" She leans on the table. Libby stares at a pile of napkins.

"Yeah, I'm fine," I say, grabbing a fork.

"J-man, do you have a crush on a girl?"

"Mom — " Libby groans, then becomes a statue again.

"What?" Soleil holds up her hands. "I can ask that. Can't I ask that, Lib?"

Libby squeezes her eyes closed like she has a headache.

"You should have stayed downstairs, then," Soleil says to Libby. "J-man, I'm just asking what's up. Any girls?"

"Nope," I say. I'd have to actually have conversations with them for that. The farthest I've gotten is to look at Rosemary Stanford from afar and imagine her talking to me. I stir my Kraft Dinner and breathe in the steamy-cheesy fumes.

Soleil shrugs. "I'm a lowly tenant, but I can't help noticing the energy in here's all off."

"The energy?"

"Yeah. Your footsteps sound — well, lonely. We just wanted to see if we could help."

Libby coughs — at least I think she does. She stares at the floor.

"I'm fine." I eat a forkful of macaroni and burn the roof of my mouth.

Soleil pulls out a chair and makes herself comfortable. "I know sad footsteps, J-man. My friend Johnny became addicted to gambling and lost all his money and then got depressed. He almost jumped off the Lion's Gate Bridge."

"That's crap," I say, even though it could totally be true.

"It is crap," Libby says from her corner. "He jumped off a ladder and broke his ankle."

"But he was practising for something bigger," Soleil says.

Libby rolls her eyes.

Soleil looks at me sadly. "J-man, I hate to see you here alone, making your poor little dinner. You want to come downstairs and watch TV with us?"

Libby looks like she wants to put her hand over her mom's mouth to stop her talking.

I do kind of want to hang out with someone and not have to think about spending a whole summer, and possibly a whole lifetime, alone. But I can't make myself say yes. Even though I know it's lame, I'd rather sit in my room and wait for an email from Grant. "No, thanks," I say.

"Okay then, suit yourself." She gets up and smooths her weird dressing gown. "We're downstairs if you need us."

Libby glances at me before she pulls open the door. "I could draw you sometime, you know. With charcoal." Then she's gone.

"We're here to help, Jakob. Your aunt's working so hard." Soleil smiles and touches my arm. She's just so *friendly*.

"Uh, thanks."

I hold my dinner in one hand and close the door behind them with the other. I watch them go down the steps and disappear under the deck. It's a little like watching a plane fade to a white dot in the sky.

Aunt Laura gets home at eight-thirty. She clunks the front door and throws her coat in the closet without hanging it up. I hear it because my room shares a wall with the hall closet.

"Jakob?"

"In my room," I call back.

She shuffles to the kitchen. "You eat?"

"Yup."

I hear her slump into a chair. "What a *day*. You?"

"Yeah."

"Three cardiac arrests in an *hour*. My shoulders are killing me." She always complains about her shoulders and back after cardiac arrests because they have to do CPR, pushing up and down on the person's chest, sometimes for hours. Sometimes she takes a sick day after, because her back seizes up. She opens and closes cupboards in the kitchen. She's forgotten about Grant leaving already. "Well, at least come out here and say hi."

I drag myself down the hall.

Aunt Laura looks like her patients. Her brown hair is greasy and she has dark circles under her eyes. It's what I assume all nurses look like. "What did you have for dinner?" she asks.

"Salad."

She looks at me suspiciously.

"Kraft Dinner," I admit.

"The staple diet of teenagers." She gets up, wincing, and goes to the kettle. "I'm making tea. You want some?"

I never want tea. I hate tea. She knows this, but always asks.

"Soleil came up," I try. It's never easy having a conversation with Aunt Laura unless it's her complaining about the hospital, with me stuck pretending to care.

"Did she? Everything okay?"

"Yeah. She wanted to hang out, I think."

"She almost got a part in a fabric softener commercial, apparently. I wonder how long she'll stick out the acting thing." Aunt Laura drops a teabag into the pot. "What about Libby?"

"What about her?"

Aunt Laura swings her head to look at me. "She come up?"

"Yeah. So?" This line of conversation's starting to make me feel a little weird.

"She probably wants to hang out. She's a cute kid."

"Exactly. Kid. She's, like, eleven."

"Actually, I think she's twelve. You were twelve last year, remember? You could use more friends, Jakob. No offence."

Yeah, because my one and only friend just left the country. "I'm kind of tired. It's been a long day," I say, trying to nudge her toward our earlier conversation.

"Oh, okay," she says, rubbing her eyes. "I'm going to have an early night myself. So many sick people today."

"Right," I say, backing out of the kitchen. She's not going to remember. Sometimes I think her brain is more switched off than mine, and I'm the one who had the head injury.

"Goodnight, then. I'm working a day shift tomorrow too, so see you same time, same place." She watches the kettle, like that will make it boil faster.

CHAPTER 2

My parents were so excited when I started high school. Like this was a milestone I might not have achieved somehow. Mom took me shopping in August and made me pick out lots of clothes. She seemed to be really worried that I not look like a loser. Dad said next summer break he'd take me camping in the Interior to study stars, just us, as a celebration of my first year in high school. I was never as interested in stars as he was. Even though his real job was an accountant, he was totally obsessed with astronomy. My mom said he wanted to name me Orion but she put her foot down. I liked the names of the constellations and the stories behind them, but he got all excited about solar flares and dwarf stars and all the statistics. There was only so much of that stuff I could listen to before I zoned out.

The best part, though, was it was just us out in the night with a telescope. I liked being around him, and I could tell he liked being around me. The night felt close and like it belonged to us somehow. *The light from that star took ten years to get here, Jakob,* he'd say. *That's some old light, eh?* When I started talking about dogs all the time, he showed me Sirius, the dog star. But that wasn't enough. I was talking about real dogs, so he bought me breed books and a DVD of *Old Yeller.* I don't think he remembered how sad the ending was. If he was disappointed that I wasn't going to be an astronomer, he didn't show it.

The problem with nighttime now is it's not just me and my dad and the stars. It's the accident. It's pieces of memory that float in my head and won't stick together in the right order. It's the dreams I have whenever I fall asleep. They start out fine — I'm with my parents somewhere, at the store or pool or eating dinner — and for a moment I let myself feel happy. But then we're in the dark car spinning off the street. We tumble. Metal screams, I scream — or is it someone else? Sticky cold on my face. Something whirring back and forth, rhythmic. I hear this so often I've started to think of it as the heart of the car, still beating, though everything else is broken. And then I'm standing on the empty street — no crumpled car, just me — with the need to search busting out of me. My feet start moving and I think if I don't find it — but what is *it?* — I will die.

And I wake up searching. Looking in my closet or halfway out of bed. But I never find what I'm looking for.

---

london is so cool, j! we have a really old house that's attached to other houses and my room is in the attic. my mom doesn't like coming up the steep stairs, so I figure I can put up my kayla marsden posters and she may never see them ;) our street has a movie theatre and a comic store w/ all the issues of dawnbreaker i couldn't find in vancouver. sucks that the end of school is lame — wish you were here so i could show you Comix. you'd love it.

grant

The last day of school should be the best day of the year. Everyone drugged on summer, with the attention span of a hamster. There's no point in me staying after my last class, so I just pack up my books, close my empty locker and count the steps to the door.

I walk home from school the long way — through the soccer fields and into the woods — so I can walk down the ravine at Mahon Park. I want to remember the times we skated until dark and walked home through the forest. Grant used to tell me about the weird things his sister, who thought she was a witch, did with her friends on weekends. They'd dress in black and speak to spirits and Grant and I would laugh until it hurt as we walked to his house or mine, planning to show up as they were going into a trance or something. His sister was our running joke.

Beside the entrance to the park is a covered board where people stick notices and ads. If I'm walking this way I usually check the board. It's kind of like reading the newspaper, but better, because things are more random and strange. One time there was a handwritten note that said, *Anyone who's seen a pink T-shirt that says "I Really Am This Gorgeous," call Maxine at 447-6947.* I told that one to my dad and he couldn't stop snorting.

This time, most of the notices are old and ripped, but there are two new ones — a lined page that asks for used clothing to be donated to some children's fund, and a small blue stickie that says: *Wanted: Daily dog walker/companion for Chilko, my four-legged buddy. Experience with dogs required. Call 554-9850.*

My heart stops. It's like someone's heard my thoughts and put this note here just for me. That's the perfect way for me to make some money and take care of a dog at the same time. If I do that all summer, Aunt Laura can't argue anymore. I get a pen and paper out of my backpack and write down the number. My hand shakes a little. This has to work. It has to.

The house is empty when I get home. I pull my phone out and go to my room to call the number from the blue stickie. There was no name on it, so I wonder who to ask for and settle on "whoever left the blue stickie in the park." I practise a few times before dialing.

The phone rings and rings on the other end, and my palms get sweatier and sweatier.

"Hello?" It's a man's low voice.

"Hi. Did you leave the blue stickie?"

"Pardon me?"

I gulp and try again. "Did you leave the blue stickie note? In the park? About the dog."

"Oh — yeah, I did. That was quick."

"It was?"

"I only left the note there two hours ago. Things move fast around here. I'm from a small town. Everything takes way longer."

I pace from the window to my bed and back. "I'm calling about walking your dog. Is it for money?"

"Uh, how old are you?"

"Thirteen — almost fourteen. I'm fit and I know the area really well. I've lived here all my life. I know dogs too — I'm kind of an expert — and I have the whole summer off."

The guy coughs on the other end. "Uh, that's a great offer, man. I'd love to take you up on that. Thing is, I need someone older to walk Chilko. He's kind of a handful. I just can't risk it — no offence — with a kid." He pauses.

"I believe you about doing a good job, though. I'm sure you would."

I sit on the bed and my stomach sinks into my shoes.

The guy clears his throat. "You there?"

"Yeah," I say.

"I'm sorry," he says. "I appreciate your interest."

I put the phone down and lie back. The faded glow-in-the-dark stars on the ceiling look ridiculous, so old and useless. I want to rip them all off and leave big, ugly holes in the paint.

"Stupid," I mutter to myself, but that makes me feel even dumber. Now I'm talking to myself like a crazy person.

I grab my pillow and throw it at my closet door, but it's a pillow and doesn't do any damage. That makes me more mad. I pick up a book and chuck it at the door. It slams and drops to the carpet. I pick up another book. It hits my swivel chair, which teeters but stays up. I push the chair over, then knock all the papers, pens and junk off my desk. I start kicking the door. And all the time I'm yelling *stupid* over and over and over until I forget what it means and who or what I'm saying it for.

Today's Most Adoptable Dog:

Hey, I'm Jackson! I'm a two-year-old border collie cross! I have so much energy, you will NEVER tire me out! Come and see me at the shelter and then take me home. I'm crate-trained!

I spend the next few days on the web, looking for dogs, jobs and ways to trade lives with someone else. I email Grant with more questions about London, but he only talks about the comic store and a skate park he found around the corner and how his sister's already meeting witches in the neighbourhood.

Soleil and Libby aren't around. In a weird way, I miss them. I miss them just being there, even if I'm not talking to them or seeing Libby's random drawings everywhere. Before they left, she pushed one through the letter slot in the front door. It was a smudged sketch of the fire hydrant outside our house.

On Monday morning, Aunt Laura makes me toast with peanut butter and a bowl of cereal for herself. She's still in her hospital scrubs from her night shift. They're light green and make her look seasick. Her face is always the most tired-looking after a night shift. When she first moved in, Aunt Laura wanted to get someone to stay the night with me. I put a stop to that because I'm old enough to take care of myself, and anyway, I'd only be sleeping. She had all kinds of reasons why I should be babysat, but I finally won. Maybe because I made her feel guilty for treating me like a kid, like my parents had. Truth was, they wouldn't have left me alone either. But she didn't know that.

"Any summer plans yet?" she asks, munching cereal.

I shrug.

"We had a kid your age in last night. Broke his jaw skateboarding."

I look up and make the appropriate surprised face.

"He'll be drinking his dinner through a straw for the next few months. Promise me you won't do something stupid like that." She reaches for the newspaper that's three days old.

"I won't do something stupid like that."

"Good."

"I have an idea, though," I say.

"For summer?"

"Sort of, yeah. I thought I could get a job. Make some money."

She examines her bowl then looks at me. "Well, that's not a bad idea. What kind of job are you thinking of?"

"I don't know. Maybe mowing lawns. Or a paper route."

She frowns. "Lawns, maybe. But I don't like the idea of you out early in this neighbourhood. You can get a paper route when you're fourteen."

"I'll be fourteen in four months. I can take care of myself."

"I know you can. You surprise me all the time."

"This is really important."

She narrows her eyes a little. That's never a good sign. "Why do you want a job so badly? What are you planning on getting?"

I stare at her soggy cereal.

"Jakob, is this still about the dog thing?"

I open my mouth to make something up, but she stops me with a hand. "We've been through that. Hasn't there been enough drama in the past six months? Do we need to add a high-maintenance animal into the mix? You've never even had one — you don't know how much work it is."

"You've never had one either," I point out.

"And I don't want to end up walking and feeding it when you get tired of it."

"That won't happen. I know how to take care of a dog. I've been researching it forever."

"Researching." She looks at me. "That's all theory, not real life."

"You sound exactly like my parents," I say.

"Probably because they were right. It's not a good idea."

"But it would help me get over it," I say, blurting out whatever comes into my head. Who knows where it's coming from.

"Get over it?" She looks a little concerned.

"You know, it would be therapeutic to prove to myself that I can do it." I try to sound like Dr. Tang, but I realize it's actually true.

Aunt Laura puts a hand on my arm. "A dog is not a psychological experiment. I'm sorry, Jakob."

I pull away. Living with her is never going to be okay.

"It's just too much right now."

"For you, maybe," I mutter.

"What?"

"What about me? I don't have any parents. I'm basically an orphan." I say it loud so it hits her in the face. "My best friend just left the country. What about me?"

She looks so sad for a moment I think I might have gotten through. But then her face crumples up in anger. "Don't talk to me about problems, Jakob. My life's been turned upside down too. I'm trying to do the best I can."

I get up and put my plate in the sink.

"You're my nephew. You mean the world to me. I understand — " She presses her fingers between her eyes. "I know we're both still grieving."

"Right. We're grieving," I say quietly. This is the point where we both look over the edge of the cliff, wondering if we should go into all the stuff we don't talk about.

"Jakob, I'm sorry. I know it's hard for you, but a dog isn't going to happen right now. Can't you see that?" And this is where she steps back, every time, so we don't have to deal with the stuff for another day. It always makes me breathe easier, but a second later I just feel angry. Like something's been grabbed out of my hands.

I head to my room, but she blocks my way. "I need to be alone now," I say to her scrubs.

She puts her hands on my shoulders. "You're a good kid. We're both just trying to figure this thing out."

"Whatever," I say. "I don't really care."

Today's Most Adoptable Dog:

Hello, I'm Buzz. I'm a Nova Scotia duck tolling retriever. I'm three years old and I love anything to do with water. If you want a best friend who can hike, swim and run with you for hours, come and take me home. I'm friendly and good with kids, and I'm well-trained. What's not to like?

I can tell Aunt Laura feels guilty about our conversation because she rents us a DVD that night and we eat my favourite, take-out sushi, on the couch. It's not a great movie, but she never gets ones I'd pick anyway.

The sushi's not bad. She lets me eat all the dynamite rolls, which are my favourite. A battle breaks out in the movie between the hero and a hairy, pig-faced bad guy. We both groan at the bad special effects.

She sighs and mutes the TV. "I've got to pee. Can you handle the suspense until I get back?"

"Somehow I'll manage." I inhale another bite of sushi.

But when she sits down again, she doesn't reach for the remote.

My jaw tenses up.

"I know this is hard, Jakob, but you really need to make some new friends this summer."

I chew my sushi slowly so I don't have to answer.

"Why don't I sign you up for a camp — baseball or tennis?"

"*Not* sports."

"Why not?"

"*Not* sports."

"Okay, what about a drama club?"

I give her a look that says are-you-kidding-me?

"Well, what then? You have to get out of the house."

"I don't want to be in a camp. They're for kids."

"Seen yourself lately?" She gets up and fills her glass at the sink. "You can't sit around here all summer."

"I get out."

"Yeah, but with other kids, I mean."

There's a knock at the back door. Soleil puts her face up to the window.

"We're not done," Aunt Laura says to me as she goes to let her in.

"Hey, upstairs neighbours." Soleil rolls into the kitchen like she's on wheels. She wears a short yellow dress that looks like it would come off if it was windy enough. It actually looks nice on her, though. Her hair's all done and she's wearing makeup. For a second I imagine what it would be like to go out with Soleil.

"Where're you off to? A film premiere?" Aunt Laura's all smiles.

"Better — a date! I haven't had one in years."

"I've forgotten what one's like," Aunt Laura says.

"Where's Libby?" I find myself saying. I wanted to say it to break up the conversation, but it comes out sounding like I care.

"She's downstairs watching an art documentary."

I snort.

"Seriously," Soleil says. "Spray paint art in a Brazilian ghetto."

"Well, she can always join us up here," Aunt Laura says. "Right, Jakob?"

"Uh, right," I mutter.

Soleil smiles at me with shiny lips. "That's really sweet. She's hard to pry away from her obsession. I'll let her know for next time. Feel free to pop down, Jakob, if you want."

"Okay, thanks," I say, thinking what I've just heard would be enough to keep anyone away.

"Hey, J-man, I wonder if you could do me a favour." Soleil comes over and sits on the couch. She smells like peach perfume.

I don't move over, even though her leg's touching mine a little. "What?"

"Tomorrow morning we're going out of town for a few days and I was hoping you could water our plants." She eats a piece of pickled ginger off my plate. "I'll pay you."

I sit up. "Really? How much?"

"You don't need to do that, Soleil," Aunt Laura says. "He'll do it any —"

"How much?" I ask again.

"Ten bucks."

"Sure. You want me to do anything else?"

"Do you mop floors?" She laughs. "Don't worry about it, J-man. The watering can will be on the counter."

"That's very nice of you, Soleil," Aunt Laura says, and offers her a cup of tea.

"Thanks, but I have to get going," Soleil says. "We'll be back by the end of the week."

She floats out and we're left with the hero of the bad movie stuck flying across the TV screen.

"Well, that'll give you one thing to do," Aunt Laura says from the sink. The dishes clatter.

I stare at the TV for a few minutes, but it's pathetic. The hero's going to beat the bad guys and rescue the girl from the coffin she's locked in. It's always the same.

"You know, I heard there's a mountain biking camp at the rec centre," Aunt Laura calls over her shoulder.

I take that as my cue to exit. "I'm going to my room," I say. "To read."

"What about the movie?"

I let her figure that one out for herself.

Mom and I are making a cake for Dad — a surprise carrot coconut cake that he'll flip over because it's his favourite and we've been really good at pretending we've forgotten his birthday. Mom's stirring in the flour and then the mustard — I know it's a dream when I ask her about the mustard and she says it's the secret ingredient. Let's eat it for dinner, *she says.* You're always asking for dessert first. *Real Mom would never do that either — vegetables are really important to her. She asks me to get the milk, but when I open the fridge door there isn't food on shelves, just a doorway onto a dark, empty street. I don't want to, but I step through, and then I'm back in the same old dream: the heartbeat of the car echoes in my head as I start the search all over again. The streets are empty, silent and still, like a photograph I'm running through. The urge is so strong it chokes me, but I run faster — I have to find* it.

I gasp for air and wake up on the floor in my room. The palms of my hands burn from the carpet.

I stand up slowly, try to focus on something other than my racing thoughts. The street lamp above Aunt Laura's car lights the rain that falls on the street. I stare out for a long time, picture myself leaving the house, running out there, actually looking. What would I find? My eyelids get heavy and I shuffle back to bed. This time I only dream of blackness.

CHAPTER 3

---

hey dude — comix doesn't have the issue of War Machines you asked about. hadn't even heard of it. i found a bunch of old x-men issues, though. i could send you some. we're going to france tomorrow to see my cousin. i hear french girls are pretty friendly if you know what i mean. you'll get my report!

I water Soleil's plants every day, Even though I know I'm not supposed to over-water them or they'll die. I snoop around her apartment a little while I'm there. She and Libby are pretty messy. Laundry is piled on her bed and there are dusty books everywhere. Libby's got games and an artist's easel, but that's about it. The suite only has one bedroom. There's a single bed behind a curtain in a corner of the living room. At first I think Libby must sleep there, but then I realize Libby's got the bedroom, right under Aunt Laura's.

Soleil's plants are really big and overgrown — one has legs made of baby plants that reach to the floor, even though it's on a stool. I call it The Thing. In the kitchen there's a jar of mini chocolate bars and I take a few. I think about watching TV down here, with the place to myself, but I can do that upstairs too — Aunt Laura's at work. I find a stack of old sketchbooks beside Libby's bed and look through them. It's mostly birds and flowers and sometimes faces, but I have to admit, she's not bad. I'm no artist, but Libby's got some talent. I just wish she didn't stalk me with it. I make sure the sketchbooks are back in the same order and in the same spot.

Each day seems to last twice as long as it should. On Wednesday I risk Aunt Laura's wrath and rearrange the glow-in-the-dark stars on my ceiling into new constellations. I just make them up, trying to remember what my dad used to say about them, but they don't stick well anymore and finally I have to toss them in the garbage. I try not to see my dad's face in my mind as I do it. I wonder how long it will take for Aunt Laura to notice the peeled-off paint. I find two new adoptable dogs — Rusty and Ben — to add to my list. Aunt Laura tries to suggest more camps and clubs, but I just walk away and eventually she stops. I build a skate ramp and practise new tricks but almost break my nose. I take a photo of my bloody face and send it to Grant. He emails back a shot of himself on a beach in France. I watch *Old Yeller* but turn it off before they have to shoot the dog.

On Thursday I wander over to Mahon Park and check the notice board. The blue stickie is gone and there are no other jobs posted. Someone's left a pair of sunglasses on the railing and I take them. On my way home I go into the corner store to buy a slushie. Grant and I used to get one for free because the people behind the counter never paid attention. I'd go up and pay for mine and Grant would sneak out with his under his shirt. Today I push my coins across the counter and watch the stocky, shaggy-haired guy drop them into the cash register. He looks like he's in high school, probably working here for the summer. For a second

I think of asking if I could get a job. How hard could it be to work at a corner store? I bet he gets free slushies.

"Uh, you okay?" The guy is staring at me.

"Yeah, fine," I mumble.

"At least you've got a summer, man. I'm stuck in here all day."

"Must suck," I say. *Do it,* I think. *Ask about a job.*

Someone brushes by me, holding out a bag of bread. "Look, I bought this yesterday and it's already mouldy."

The guy gives me a look, then peers at the bread. "You-can-exchange-it-or-get-a-refund-with-a-receipt."

I shuffle back into the hot sun.

On Friday Soleil and Libby come home and give me the ten dollars, plus a huge chocolate bar from wherever they went. I feel bad for eating the mini chocolate bars in their jar — all week I've been taking a few and it's half empty now. Soleil doesn't seem to have noticed. Aunt Laura pours her tea and they chat while I channel-surf through the usual crap.

"Jakob really enjoyed helping out with the plants," Aunt Laura tells Soleil. "He was down there every day."

"That's so nice of you, J-man," Soleil calls from the kitchen. "You can be my perpetual plant-waterer."

"He needs to get into a club or something," Aunt Laura tells her. "I tried to talk to him about the rec centre's camps. I'm worried about him here the *whole* summer."

"I can hear you," I call back, and flick past some cooking show where they're boiling lobsters. It gives me the creeps.

"It's not a secret," Aunt Laura says. "You're moping around here — "

"I'm not moping."

"You are. You're sulking."

Soleil makes a *tsk* sound. "Libby'd be happy to hang out you know, J-man. She's home from art camp in the afternoons."

Aunt Laura tries to sound encouraging. "That's an idea. You guys could go to the pool or ride your bikes to the corner store."

I stare at the weather guy explaining tomorrow's highs. "No thanks. I'm fine."

"Jakob, don't be rude. Couldn't you show Libby around? She's still new here — "

"Oh my god," I mutter. "Just leave me alone." I throw the remote down and stomp to my room, slamming the door. At least that feels good.

It's dark and cool in here because the curtains are drawn. Day number eight of the summer that lasted forever. I leave the light off and sit on my bed, wondering what I should do. Go on the internet? Read? Go to sleep? Dig a tunnel into the middle of the earth? Nothing sounds good.

Aunt Laura knocks on my door. "Jakob?"

"I'm sleeping."

"We should talk about this," she says.

Talk? You never want to talk.

I hear her sigh. "I have to cover a night shift for someone tonight. You'll be okay?"

"Fine."

Soon I hear the front door close and her car start up. I fumble around and find a flashlight in my bedside table and turn it on. The batteries are almost done. I watch the beam move over my closet, my computer screen, the closed door. I sit there until it fades out and dies.

We're making a snowman, the three of us, and Dad's found a top hat and fancy-looking cane for it. I have no idea where he got those but I don't ask because I know I'm dreaming this. Around us, kids make snowmen with their parents — there must be dozens of families and dozens of snowmen in the park. Then I see it from above, as if I'm flying. Ours is the only one with a top hat. I'm looking for my parents among the families below when the snow starts to melt and everything goes brown, then black, and I hit the ground. Another strange, dark street and I'm wondering what just happened, but the need to search feels like it will burst out of my chest.

I wake up with the scratchy carpet on my cheek. My clock radio says 12:36. I pull open the curtains. It's a full moon out there, lots of light to see by. There are shadows on the street from the cars and telephone poles. A full moon means you can see a lot better than other times of the month, but it also means weird things happen. Aunt Laura always says the worst injuries come into Emerg on a full moon. It's like something happens to people's brains — they act crazier than normal. And animals do too. The coyotes come out of Mahon Park and howl at the full moon.

Out on the street, something catches my eye. It's a dog, a big grey and white one, trotting along the sidewalk. It stops to sniff a metal pole and then pees on it.

I open my window to see better and the frame creaks. The dog hears it, pricks his ears.

"Psst." I stick my head out the window. "Over here."

The dog turns and fixes his eyes on me. His tail wags a

little. Just at the white tip. There's no one else around, no owner that I can see.

Something inside me makes a decision. Actually, it's someone: J, the guy who tried the highest rails on my skateboard and told Grant the dirtiest jokes. J says it's time to go. I close my window and grab my hoodie from the closet. It's not cold out, but I feel better having it. The hair on my neck stands up as I shuffle down the hall and take the quietest route through the kitchen to the back door. The floors are old and creaky and even though Aunt Laura's not here, I don't want Soleil or Libby to hear me. I grab my key from the bowl, close the door as slowly as I can and lock it behind me. The steps down from the deck are creaky too, so I take the first two and then jump past the rest, onto the crusty grass. There are no lights on in Soleil's place.

My skin feels cool and prickly. It's finally happening. No more running around while I'm asleep. I sneak around the side of the house and open the gate. But what if the dog's gone — or what if I imagined him? A memory flashes through my mind so fast I can't catch it. It seems really familiar somehow, watching a dog out at night, but I can't think why. Maybe it'll come to me if I find him.

When I get to the pole I saw him pee on, he's not far away, sniffing in our neighbour's flowerbed. He looks like a wolf, but I'm sure he's a husky. A girl in my grade seven class had one and it looked like this. Black and grey on top and white on the belly, with face markings like a wolf, and a grey tail with a white tip. His ears are black and they stick straight up, like fuzzy triangles. I want to feel how soft they are. Huskies sometimes come into the shelters, but lately they've been adopted really fast. I had one, Rex, on my list last month but he was gone in two days.

I stand there waiting, watching to see if he'll run when he sees me, but he keeps sniffing, and his tail starts to wag like he's found something good.

I walk closer. He scratches the dirt with his paw and pees on the spot. When he's finished he looks really proud of himself and turns around to face me, like he knew I was there all along. We stare at each other.

"Hi," I say.

He smells the air.

"Where are you going?" I ask. I look back at my house to make sure no lights are on. Everything is quiet, except for one or two cars passing on the main road a few streets over.

The dog turns and walks down the sidewalk, slowly, not like he's running away, but like he's going for a stroll. I follow. He stays in front of me, sniffing the grass and flowers, but I get the feeling he's sensing me too. When he gets to the corner, he waits.

"Can I come?" I ask. It's pretty stupid to ask a dog questions. "I'm J," I say, because that's who I'll be tonight. I'm not Jakob Nobody or Jakob Nebedy. Not even J-man. I'm J, and tonight I'm going to do whatever I want.

The dog looks up the street and then crosses. We leave my house behind.

We walk down the middle of the boulevard, along the street that leads to the grocery store and then down the hill, toward the harbour. I haven't been out this late since my dad took me camping in Manning Park and we stayed up to watch the stars. That's when he told me about Sirius, the dog star. Brightest in the sky. I paid attention when he talked about it because it's in Canis Major, the big dog constellation.

I thought it might be cool to name my dog Sirius. Now,

as I look for it, I think it's perfect that there's a giant dog in the sky looking down at me — a tiny moving speck on a small street.

We walk down Mahon Avenue in the middle of the night. I feel alive. I feel bright somehow. The dog's bouncing along ahead of me and a few cars drive past, but no one stops or honks or seems surprised there's a kid walking around this late. I guess if I look like I have somewhere to be, like I belong here, no one cares. I'm tall for my age, and with my hood pulled up, maybe I can pass for older. I take bigger steps. It starts to feel like I imagined it would.

We walk all the way to the Quay, where the tug boats and ferries are moored. The dog doesn't come up to me, but he stays close, and if I get too slow he waits for me. He pees on *everything*. I wonder what would happen if I peed on something, and since I have to go anyway, I step behind a tree and pee on the trunk. The dog turns around to see what I'm doing. He sniffs the spot for a long time.

"I know marking with pee is really important for dogs, but you're kind of obsessive."

As if to reply, he lifts his leg and pees right next to my spot.

"What's your name?" I ask him. There's no collar around his neck. Maybe he's a stray.

He looks across the street to the empty parking lot in front of the water. I haven't been down here in a long time, not since last time I took the Seabus, when Aunt Laura and I went to see an Imax movie downtown. It was her first try at us doing something together, and even though the movie was a lame animation, I pretended to like it. She pretended to like it too and we had this weird conversation where we tried to act like we enjoyed it when it was obvious neither of us did.

Now there's a new pier beside the parking lot, reaching out into the sea, and the dog heads for it. He trots across the road like there's no worry about cars — and there aren't many this late, but I wonder what happens during the day, if he's ever been hit. Some dogs just don't understand cars.

I follow him across the parking lot and we walk down the pier. He jumps onto the short cement wall and trots along it, glancing into the water. He's just so sure of himself. Like I want to be — confident and not afraid of anything. Cool.

I jump up too and we look out over the black ocean, toward downtown and the lights of the skyscrapers. They're way brighter down here, not dim and twinkly like they are from my house. I guess it's a little like stars — it depends where you're seeing them from.

The dog comes to the end of the pier and jumps off the wall. He sniffs around for a while, but I stay up there, watching the ocean. Suddenly a dark round head comes up from the water.

"Hey!" I shout.

I feel a breeze beside me and the dog's there, looking over the side too. It's like he's saying, *What is it?*

"Over there." I motion out on the water.

The head bobs, and then I see it's got a snout. A seal.

The dog sniffs the air, staring at the seal too. He leans a little over the edge.

"Whoa, don't fall in," I say. I put my hand on his back, the coarse fur on top. It's cool on my skin, but underneath, the soft fur is warm. I wish we could just stand there together, but after a minute he jumps down again. He felt so solid.

I look back at the way we've come. From here I can see all the way up the hill — the main street with lights along it and houses on both sides. Some have lights on but most don't. I try to figure out where mine would be. I'm getting a little cold standing still, even with my hoodie on. I stick my hands in my pockets.

The dog trots back up the pier. I've never had so many questions for something that can't answer me. Where does he live? Is he a stray? He looks pretty well cared for and well-fed. Does he have nice owners who are looking for him right now? How is he going to find his way home?

We walk back up the hill, sort of in the direction of my house. My watch says 1:52. This dog must have super strength and never need to sleep. He walks with his tail flagging the air, and even though he's got almost no pee left, he still lifts his leg and lets a tiny dribble come out.

"Where to now?" I ask. I'm not ready to go home, but a place to sit and rest would be nice. And I could handle a sandwich or something. My stomach growls.

I sit on some steps leading to an apartment building.

A car drives by with really loud rap blaring and someone yells out of the window at us. A hoarse voice carries through the air above the thumping bass: "Hey, kid — does your mommy know you're not in bed?" It has the opposite effect on J than it would on me. J yells back, "Does your mother know you're a pathetic loser?" I yell even after they've turned the corner. It feels so good to fill my lungs with breath and spit out words like that.

The dog stops scratching his ear and looks at me. His eyes are orangey brown in the streetlight.

"That's how it's done," I say to him. "See that? No more boring, invisible Jakob!"

"Hey!"

I jump up.

Someone's leaning out of an apartment window. A man

with no shirt on. "Keep it down, kid. Go home and act crazy there."

I take a step to leave, but J comes roaring back. "It's a free world!" I yell.

He holds out his phone. "Oh yeah? There's cops around here who'll tell you different. Want me to call them?"

"Uh, no thanks!" I say, and sprint up the street, the dog at my heels. I think we both got a kick out of that.

I can't believe J just did that — and got away with it. I feel light, lighter than air. I never want to go home.

The dog takes a left onto Sixth Street and sniffs around in the bushes. He comes out chomping something, probably garbage from someone's patio, but it reminds me that I'm starving.

I head down the street in the direction of my house, and the dog comes too, but after a block he wants to cross the street.

"I'm this way," I say, pointing. "I'm going to grab some food. You know food? Treats?"

His ears prick up. He knows treats.

I have to be careful around our house. Even though it's two in the morning, anyone could be looking out their windows. If it was me, I'd keep the dog away, go home and call it a lucky, awesome night, but J pushes the gate open and lets the dog into the backyard. The dog bounds around the dry grass, his tail flying, and I grab him in case Soleil's awake.

I start for the stairs. The dog sees where I'm going and tries to get up there first, but I hold him by the shoulders. He's got a lot of muscle under that coat. Reminds me that he's an animal, a wolf cousin. And I don't know him that well. He looks up at me.

"Your claws will make too much noise on the floor," I whisper. "You can't come in — someone might hear you."

I look around for something to tie him up with. Since he's not wearing a collar, I'll need something pretty long. In a bucket under the deck, I find the rope Aunt Laura uses as a laundry line. I tie it around his neck and then around the railing of the stairs. He pulls a little but it holds.

"Stay there for a minute. I'll be back." I tiptoe up the stairs and unlock the door. The dog looks up at me with his fuzzy triangle ears pointing to the sky. He stays.

Inside I grab a granola bar and look for something to give him. I settle on cheese, since the only other thing is bacon, and it's raw and Aunt Laura would definitely be suspicious if uncooked bacon disappeared in the middle of the night. Maybe I'll buy a bag of dog treats and keep it in my room in case the dog comes back. I've already decided he will.

I sneak back outside and feed him his treat. He gobbles it down without even chewing it and sniffs for more. I eat my granola bar sitting on the first step with his eyes following my every move. He's almost as tall standing up as I am sitting down. He sniffs my hands for granola crumbs. His nose is cold and wet and his whiskers tickle my palm. The tips of his ears are like puppy fur. He lets me pet them for a moment. I get the feeling he doesn't let everyone do that.

Then a light comes on behind me in a window under the deck. My heart skids to a stop and I dive off the stairs, pulling the dog with me, out of view. Shielded by the pile of junk under the deck, I squint at the little square of window I can see between a watering can and a stack of wood. Soleil moves around the kitchen with a teapot. What is she doing up at this hour? I realize I'm gripping the laundry rope around the dog's neck and let it go a little. The dog tries to get up and I whisper to him, "Just stay for a second — if she sees you we'll be dead!"

Soleil glances at something on the windowsill. She grabs the phone and dials. Finally she leaves the kitchen and I decide it's our time to make a move — who knows when she'll be back.

I squat beside the dog and untie him. "We've got to get out of here. You have to follow me, okay?"

The dog doesn't need any convincing. He leaps when I let him go and we race across the yard toward the gate, except he gets there way before I do, and just as I reach to pull the gate closed behind me, Soleil's door opens.

"Jakob?"

I freeze with my back to the voice, watching the dog, safe on the street, watching me. He waits to see if I'm coming. I motion for him to go, get out of here. There's no saving me now. I turn.

"Jakob, what are you doing?" It's not Soleil. Libby stands in the doorway in yellow pyjamas and a black sweater.

My mind races. Think: what am I doing?

She pushes the hair out of her face, looking half asleep. "I thought I saw something in the backyard. Why are you out here?"

"What are *you* doing up?" I say before I can stop J from speaking. But it buys me some thinking time.

She looks surprised. "I couldn't sleep. Mom's making tea and we're watching TV. What about you?"

J has the words ready just in time. "I saw something out here. I think it was a raccoon. I came out to see — it went through the gate." I point, hoping the dog is long gone.

Libby pulls her sweater tighter and closes the door behind her. "Is that what it was?"

"Yup." I close the gate, glancing to the street, and there's no sign of the dog.

Libby looks suspicious. "How could you see a raccoon in the back yard from your bedroom? Your window faces the street, like mine."

I walk slowly toward the stairs, trying to look insulted. "I heard it. Didn't you? You think I'm lying?"

She leans against the doorframe and crosses her arms. "Uh huh."

I have no idea what she'll say next. I just want to get upstairs and inside. "What do you know? I've heard raccoons before. I know what they sound like."

Libby gives me a long stare. "You think I'm stupid."

Maybe it would have been easier if Soleil had seen me. "No, I never said that."

"You were doing something else, I know it. You were running away."

I hold out my hands and at least I can be honest about this. "No way, Libby. I was not running away." At least, not running far.

She doesn't look like she buys it.

"Look, I don't care if you believe me. I saw what I saw."

She lifts her chin. "Heard, you mean."

"Heard too. Man, you're like a bloodhound." This is the most I've ever heard her say. I take another step and hope she's getting the hint to go back inside.

"Jakob?"

"Yeah?" I turn.

She's standing at the bottom of the stairs, holding the noose on the end of the laundry rope that minutes ago was around the dog's neck. She gathers it and throws it back into the bucket. "Goodnight."

CHAPTER 4

The next day I'm lying on a towel in the backyard after lunch, reading an X-Men comic for the twentieth time, when Soleil comes out of the suite. She's wearing a red dress and pointy shoes and her hair is wavy. She's got a weird work schedule I can't figure out, and considering she's a dog groomer, she has a weird uniform too. But I'm not complaining.

"Hey, J-man," she says and hunches down beside me in the grass. "Whatcha reading?"

I flip the cover over so she can see.

"Hmm. Looks violent. Lots of blood and gore?"

I lean on my elbow. "Nah. It's kind of boring. I've read it a million times."

"I bet you're a super-fast reader."

I shrug, thinking she means because I have nothing better to do. "You got an audition?"

"Job interview," she says. "I'm looking for something better than the dog groomer's. There's only so much shampoo and nail clipping one can take." She smiles down at me.

"Where's Libby?"

Soleil's eyebrows go up. "Well, since you asked, that's what I wanted to talk to you about."

I sit up, worried. "It is?"

"There's been some, uh, problems with Libby's summer

camp." She waves her hand. "Stuff I won't bore you with — but today is her last day there. I'm letting her stay home for a while."

"I could have told you camps were trouble," I say, though I'm curious what the "problems" are.

"Yeah, well it's not Libby, I can tell you that. Some people's kids . . . " She looks over the fence at something.

I wait, not sure what to say next.

"Anyway." She shakes her head. "I already talked with Laura, but I wanted to ask you before I said anything to Libby. Could she hang out with you? Only for a little while, maybe a week or two at the most. It would help me out so much, J-man."

No. No way. I will not babysit a kid who got kicked out of a lame art camp and who might have evidence against me. I stare at the grass, trying to think of a way to let her down.

"J-man, I'm really counting on you. Libby likes you, I can tell, and I'd rather not leave her alone. It's just until I get things sorted out with work."

"I don't know," I mumble.

"Look, I know it's not ideal, but I trust you. I know you're a responsible kid."

"I don't babysit," I say, lying back down on my stomach.

"That's fine — you don't need to babysit her, she's twelve. You're just hanging out."

A thought comes into my head. I look up at Soleil. She's got a desperate look on her face.

"But say I was sort of babysitting. I'd be getting, you know, money." The instant I say it, I feel bad, knowing she's looking for a job.

Soleil looks over the fence again. "You're right. Of course."

"It's just, I mean — " I don't know what I mean. I wish she'd leave and I could go back to my comic like nothing happened.

"I can't afford a lot, Jakob, but how's thirty bucks for a week, starting tomorrow?"

I stop mumbling. I could have enough money to adopt a dog by the end of the summer. And I'll be showing more responsibility.

"Sure," I say. " I'll do it."

A few hours later I find out how Libby feels about this new arrangement.

"This sucks, Mom!" I hear her shout downstairs. Their windows are open, like ours, because it's so hot. I had no idea Libby even had a loud setting.

Soleil says something I can't make out.

"But he doesn't like me. He thinks I'm a loser."

"No, he doesn't. I'm sure he thinks you're wonderful."

"Not wonderful, Mom. And I don't need to be babysat."

"It's not babysitting," Soleil says.

I lean out my window to hear better.

"Are you paying him?" Libby asks.

"That's not the point. You can't go back to camp and I can't leave you alone. That's the end of it."

"*He* stays alone all day. Why can't I?"

"Doesn't it seem a little silly to have both of you alone but in the same house? Libby, there is no negotiation here."

"I can't believe this." A door slams. Her bedroom door.

"Lib."

I can hear Soleil knocking on the door. "Lib, open up. I just don't want it to be like last time, okay? I'm trying to protect you."

I don't hear the door open and Soleil doesn't say anything else.

---

j, that's a crazy story about the dog. maybe you can keep it if no one owns it. did you mean you walk him at night? must be awesome to explore in the dark. hope you don't get mugged lol! france is definitely great — by france I mean girls. i'll fill you in when i'm home.

> *My mom sits on the couch, shelling peanuts into a bowl, as I tell her what the kids have been calling me at school.* Nobody wants to play, and nobody wants to be Nobody's friend! *She hands me a peanut and it grows in my palm until it's an apple. Another weird dream. I take a bite.* They're just kids, *she says.* They have no idea how great you are. Just hang around people who do. *I want to tell her that hanging around my parents all the time isn't a lot of fun, but I don't want to hurt her feelings. She reaches out to touch my face.*

The shriek of my alarm makes me bolt out of sleep. Midnight. I slam the snooze button and look out the window. The dog's not there.

I stand with my head out of the window for twenty minutes, listening to every little sound on the street. A few cars drive by. A cat screeches behind someone's house. A waft of skunk hits my nose and makes me want to gag. Maybe the cat got sprayed. You have to watch it around here with skunks.

Twenty-five minutes and the dog still hasn't shown up. I start to get the feeling he's not coming. Maybe he roams a different place every night. Maybe he got locked inside. Then a thought hits me: maybe he got picked up by the pound. I think about turning on my computer to look up the pound's number, but just then I see a shape moving on the other side of the street.

It's him.

My chest tightens as I hold my breath — a flash of memory runs across my brain so fast I can't chase it. This dog definitely triggers something. I scramble for my hoodie. J is back and ready to go.

The air is a little cooler than last night so I'm glad I brought a tuque. I sneak behind the neighbours' bushes so there's less chance to be seen. The dog waits on the sidewalk, his tail wagging. It's a bigger wag than last time and I take that to mean he remembers last night. It's almost like he's picked me — I'm the winner.

"Good to see you too," I say, and squat down beside him. He comes close and sniffs my hand. I stroke his back, feel the layers of thick fur. He lets me pet him for a minute but then he trots away, like he's saying, *Come on, let's get out of here.*

Then I notice a collar around his neck. "Hey, wait," I say. "Let me see that."

The dog stops and watches me. His ears are up in listening position.

He stays and I grab the band, looking for a tag. There's a blue plastic circle with a name printed on it and a phone number: *Chilko 554-9850.*

Chilko. My hands freeze.

The dog tugs to get away and keeps going down the road,

looking back to see if I'm coming. This is the dog from the blue stickie — I know it. How many dogs are named Chilko?

My mind races. He must live close — maybe even down the street. The owner on the phone said they just moved to town. I haven't noticed any moving vans or for sale signs around here.

But should I take him, knowing that he's escaped from his owner's yard? Of course, J says. He's here to roam. It's his owner's fault that he got out in the first place.

The dog — Chilko — is waiting by a driveway. Finally my feet wake up and I start walking. Then I start jogging. Chilko thinks it's a game and takes off at full speed ahead of me. I pull into a run and it feels good. Chilko paces me, almost smiling.

It's all laid out for us. Tonight we're going to search for the place I see every night in my head. Who knows — maybe Chilko's even the key to unlocking my memory. I won't wake up with that helpless, disappointed feeling because I'm out looking for real. And even though I still don't know what I'm looking for, if I look hard enough, I might just find it. We break into a sprint and launch off the curb into the empty street.

After a while, running gets sweaty and tiring, so we walk. Toward the water again, but the way we get there is new. Chilko wants to take some back alleys. We get off the main road and onto a gravel lane behind a bunch of houses. It's not illegal or trespassing, but I feel a little strange walking past people's old cars and garbage cans and stacks of newspapers. It's all the stuff you don't see from the front, the personal stuff. J thinks it's pretty cool to check out people's secrets. Only here it's in the open, spread out like a garage sale. Chilko trots ahead, sniffing and peeing on telephone poles, trees, bushes and even car tires. I look into every yard to see if there are lights on in the houses. A few are, but no one looks out at us. I'm glad I wore my grey hoodie for camouflage.

Suddenly there's a scratching sound and a cat launches past me in the other direction. Chilko's seen it and charges back, his legs blurring underneath him. I had no idea he could run so fast. The cat shoots into a small hole in the side of a garage and Chilko gets there a second too late — and rams into the garage. The whole thing shudders. He looks a little startled, and walks away unsteadily. He glances at me proudly as he trots by, his tail high and waving.

After I'm done laughing, I look around to make sure no one's coming out to check on the noise, but everything's still. I follow Chilko out of the alley and onto Third Street.

As he checks out everything for new smells, I try to find Sirius. First I have to find Canis Major, the big dog, and after a few minutes, I think I have. My dad could always point them out way before I found them. *Years of obsession,* he said. *It's like rereading my favourite book.* The constellation doesn't look like a dog at all, but Dad said most of them don't really look like their names. You have to draw lines between the stars to get why they were called the hunter or big bear. And even then, it's hard to see the shape.

We cross another street, into an area I've never explored before. Chilko takes a left to follow a good smell. I call to him and he turns his head. But then he keeps going.

That's when a cop car pulls around the corner. I duck behind a hedge. The car moves in slow motion, riding along the curb behind Chilko, and he doesn't notice, just keeps on sniffing. I hope the hedge hides me enough, then call him loudly, but the cop is getting out of the car and Chilko's seen him. He thinks the cop's friendly.

I hold my breath as the cop leans down and pets Chilko, gets a tail-wag. Then he grabs Chilko's collar and looks at the tag — pulls out his phone and starts dialling.

I don't think — just scramble out of the hedge and make as much noise as I can, waving my hands and calling Chilko's name. He strains at the cop's grip, and the cop is surprised enough to let go.

"Hey — is that your dog? Wait!" he yells, starting to run after Chilko. "Do you live here? Stop!"

I don't stop. Chilko reaches me and we sprint together down the sidewalk, turn the corner, not looking back. I hear the cop rev his engine and drive after us, but we take a left and double back into an alley. I scan the dumpsters and parked cars for a place to hide. Chilko runs ahead, loving the game. "In here," I tell him, and we duck into a garage that stinks like pee and rotten food. My hand touches something sticky.

Tires crunch gravel as the cop car slowly drives past us. The guy's on the radio, answering a crackling voice. I press myself into the concrete and try not to think about the sticky stuff I'm covered in. Chilko shifts beside me, his ears forward. I reach for his shoulder in case I need to hold him back. Touching his fur makes everything a little less crazy.

Suddenly blue and red lights flash into the garage — blue-red, blue-red — and then the tires squeal and the cop car spins out of the alley, turning on its siren as it takes the corner. Chilko moans, then breaks into a howl as the siren fades.

"Bad timing," I whisper, waving my hand in his face.

"We're trying to hide here."

He closes his mouth, swallowing the sound, then gets up to explore the garage.

I sit in my sticky spot for a few minutes, just trying to breathe normally as Chilko sniffs around the dumpsters.

I step out and look at my hand — brown goopy slime coats it. I can't bring myself to smell it, but from here it looks like nothing I want on my body. Got to find some grass to wipe it on.

When my hand is mostly clean, I straighten up and look around. The neighbourhood is quiet. I strain to listen for a far-off siren, anything. We're alone. We got away.

J rises up, filling my head with his roar. I jump in the air, making Chilko bounce on his feet, not sure what kind of game this is. We escaped a cop. It was *so close*. Grant won't believe me when I tell him. I'm too excited to think about a plan, so we walk farther from the alley and I try to take deep breaths. My hands shake so much I have to put them in my pockets. Chilko trots along like nothing happened. Just another adventure.

I replay the whole scene over and over and by the time I check the next street sign, I realize we're far from where I thought we were. Cygnet Street. The name sounds familiar but I don't know why. Big, dark houses. Lines of parked cars. I look up to find Sirius, and it's in the same spot, as if we haven't moved at all. The sky's so big that we basically haven't.

Something's nudging me about the street name. Cygnet. I close my eyes. *That's a constellation, Jakob.* My dad's voice pulls me back. I'm in the car, he's driving, Mom's in the passenger seat. We're going on Christmas vacation. *Cygnus is the swan,* Dad said as he turned this corner, on this exact street. *It's easier to see in the summer. We can look for it when we go camping in July.* I wasn't really listening — I'd heard it all before. He said it had another name too, something about a cross. I stare at the street sign, then up in the sky. I don't even know what Cygnus looks like. I'll never find it just standing here.

Chilko sneezes beside me.

A piece of the puzzle just dropped out of the sky but I have no idea where to go from here. I wish I could remember. "Let's go," I mutter. "This is stupid."

We walk two more blocks along Cygnet Street but nothing gets more familiar. I get grumpier. How am I ever going to find anything like this? My eyes feel sandy. It's 2:15. At the next intersection, I turn left, then left again. Chilko follows silently. By the time we get back to my neighbourhood, I'm counting the steps to my computer. Research. I can't walk the whole city at this pace. I need a map. And my dad's star chart. He never would have thought I'd use it for anything, especially not this.

A block from where we met, Chilko crosses the road.

"Where are you going?" I ask, but then it's obvious. He's going home. Wherever that is. We meet, we roam, we go home. He's my partner. I give him a wave and watch him slip around the corner. For a moment I want to run after him. He's so much smarter than me — knows how to travel, how to take care of himself. Doesn't get worried or scared. Just lives.

CHAPTER 5

---

hey j, you're having some crazy nights, sounds like. kinda wish it had happened when i was still there. i don't really get what you mean about the stars — isn't the northern cross a medal they give soldiers? i'm going out to skate with this guy i met next door. you'd like him. he's from Germany. ttyl

---

I'm in another boring social studies class trying to focus on the teacher's droning voice when I look over and Dad's sitting at the desk beside me. He's all hunched over as if he's writing a note. It looks so ridiculous, I laugh. No one else looks up. Dad, *I say.* What are you doing here? *He glances at me, hiding whatever he's writing with his arm.* Hey, Jakob. Thought I'd try school again, *he says. He's not doing a great job of it if he's already goofing off in class, but I don't have time to tell him this. Someone taps me on the back of the head. I almost jump out of my seat when I see my mom sitting behind me.* Hi, sweetheart, *she says.* Having a good day? *I look back to see the teacher motioning me to the front of the class, a stern look on his face. As I take the ten steps to the board, it turns into an open window looking onto a dark street — here we go again. I don't even look back to see if my parents are still sitting in the class. I just climb through the window and hit the ground running. Nothing seems familiar — until I see a street sign with no words, just a picture of a swan. That's new. I run past it and far off, a siren sounds. Not a police car, an ambulance, more than one. The heartbeat of the car fills my ears and my chest is tight. I turn in circles trying to find the right way. I look so hard I wake myself up.*

Bumps and thuds echo from the kitchen: 8:54.

"Morning," Aunt Laura says as I emerge, dressed and yawning. I must look like I thought it was a school day, but really I didn't want to sit in sweaty pyjamas for breakfast.

"So today's the day," she says, putting toast onto a plate.

"For what?" I ask.

"Libby. Your new friend?"

"She's not my friend."

"Right. She's your summer buddy." Aunt Laura hands me the jam.

"God, stop it. She's nothing, okay?"

"But you're doing it."

"Doing what? You make it sound so weird."

She sighs, hands me a knife as I stick my finger into the jam. "You're looking after Libby. Like you promised Soleil."

"Whatever." I spread too much jam on my toast, the way I like it. "It's temporary. Soleil said until she found work."

Aunt Laura looks at me. "Gee, Jakob. It's not like you've got anything better to do."

I glare at her.

"Just treat her nicely, okay? That's all I ask." Aunt Laura rubs her eyes. "She might actually be someone who understands what it means to be alone."

Libby comes out of the basement suite with a pad of paper and a box of pencils, sets them up at the picnic table and starts drawing. Her long black skirt hides her feet and drags on the ground. There's a bright orange gypsy-looking thing around her shoulders. I really don't get how girls choose their clothes.

I stay on my side of the yard, half-pretending to read a book about stars. The other day I found out that Cygnus is also called the Northern Cross, which makes it much easier to find because it's cross-shaped.

"You don't have to talk to me," Libby says suddenly. She stares at her paper.

"I'm not," I say, stating the obvious.

"But for the rest of the day. You can just do whatever. I'll pretend you're not there if you want."

"I don't care." She's making me uncomfortable, but it's my yard, so I refuse to leave. We both go back to what we were doing — or in my case, not doing.

A car blasting rock music drives past the house. It's the Cosmic Turkeys, a band Grant loved — "Water From Stone," from their second album. I whisper the lyrics under my breath until the car takes the music away.

"You know that song?" Libby asks.

"I thought we weren't talking," I say.

"I said you didn't *have* to talk to me. If you want to, you can. It's a personal choice."

"Well, I choose not to. You know, out of respect. You asked *me* the question."

She takes her eyes off whatever she's drawing. "You know, I thought you were kind of cool when I first met you."

"Let me guess. That's all changed?"

She rolls her eyes, goes back to her drawing.

The sun bakes me inside my clothes until it feels like I'll melt right here on the grass. I need water — cold, with ice.

"You want a drink?" I ask, forgetting we're not supposed to be talking.

She looks up, startled. "Yeah. Thanks. With ice, please."

I stumble across the lawn, a little dizzy. From behind her, I get a glimpse of a drawing that fell out of her sketchbook.

I stop. "What's that?" I try to keep my voice steady. It's not perfect, but a creepy-close drawing of a black and white husky.

"It's a dog," she says. "Doesn't it look like one?"

"Well, I wasn't sure," I say, to cover my shock.

"Are you just going to stand there staring into space?"

I take a few steps back, not sure what to do next.

"You know, people think I'm weird but you're kind of freaky yourself," she says.

I shrug, turn toward the house. How does she know Chilko? I'm positive it's him on the page. I bet she'd tell if I asked. *No way,* J thinks. *She's not trustworthy. She'll ask questions.*

"I should show you how to draw," Libby says. Her voice sounds far away in my brain.

"No, thanks," I mutter, while J tries to convince me not to say anything else.

"Well, I'm drawing you next," she says, flipping to a fresh piece of paper.

I stare at her. She's looking through her box for the right pencil.

"I'm not posing," I say.

"I didn't ask you to. I know what you look like."

"That's creepy."

"Why? It's not a nude study."

I shudder as I slowly take the steps. My head aches a little from this strange conversation.

By the time I come back out with the water the questions are piling up inside me. There's a drawing of Chilko over there. Did she see him that night he was in the yard? I was sure he got out before she saw him, but maybe . . .

She's concentrating so hard, she doesn't even notice me. Her hair has fallen in front of her face. I have no idea how she can even see what she's doing. I put her glass on the table and lie down beside my book. Even with my eyes closed I see the drawing of Chilko, the rope she held up after he escaped.

Someone clears their throat. Libby's looking down at me. Up close I can see freckles on her nose. Her eyes are pale blue. She stares at me, waiting.

"What?"

"I asked if you wanted to see your portrait."

"It's done?"

"It's just a sketch. I wanted to capture you quickly."

The way she says *capture* makes me squirm. No wonder she has no friends.

When I don't reply, she holds the paper over my face.

I take it and sit up. Before I can say anything, she's sitting cross-legged beside me.

"It's the way I saw you the other night when you were out here."

It's a figure, blurred around the edges, with an oversized head and huge eyes. But they are my eyes. The face looks surprised, like it's been caught doing something. Behind it to the right is a street lamp, a stream of light coming down to the ground. On the other side of me is a coil of rope. If I was a stranger looking at this, I might think the figure was going to hang himself or something. Is that what she thinks? I'm glad there's no dog in the picture but I can't help feeling she knows too much. Maybe not from seeing Chilko that night, but it seems too much to be a coincidence. I don't want to see the next thing she draws.

"What do you think?"

"It's original. Different," I say. I'm surprised my voice works.

"Carmen Rosemont says most people don't understand true art. She doesn't show her work to any friends or family — just has it in galleries and strangers and critics love it." She shrugs. "I don't care if you don't like it. That's not the point."

"What is the point?" I don't say that I'm not a friend or family member and I don't ask who Carmen Rosemont is.

She gets up, sweeps the paper from my hand. "The point is to tell a story. Even one that lasts a second. That's the story of you the other night."

I can't argue with that. In fact, I can't really say anything. So I just stare into the sky until my eyes water from the brightness and I have to close them.

A while later, from across the yard, she says, "I'm going inside now. You don't have to babysit me, Jakob. I'll tell Mom we got along great."

I want to apologize for something but I don't know what. Instead I say, "Fine."

She walks across the grass with her paper and pencil box, pauses at the door. "But I do wish we got along great, you know."

She turns inside, leaving me feeling like a loser, wanting to ask her for the drawing just so I can pretend I like it when it really weirds me out and I don't want to look at it ever again. I realize why: it's too true. The eyes, the rope. It was full of guilt, being caught in the act. It *was* the story of that second, whether she knew what happened or not.

CHAPTER 6

Midnight. Chilko and I meet silently out front, a well-practiced team, and cruise down the street like ghosts. J's ready to run and he's sure it's going to be a good night. I printed out a map and traced where I think we've been already. Cygnet Street seemed even more important when I saw it on paper, but beyond that nothing stood out. I need to walk the neighbourhoods. I feel so much closer to knowing with a map and my backpack filled with water, food, a flashlight, and Chilko beside me. He glances at me with those dark orange eyes. I could hug him, but I know that's not his style.

The blip of a siren heads in the opposite direction a street over, but I automatically duck behind a tree. This is the training I need: street smarts. How to move around and not get caught. I'm so wrapped up in plans for making myself invincible that I don't notice Chilko. He's stopped. We're at the edge of Victoria Park, which is just lawns and flowers and benches that old people sit on during the day. But tonight there's something in there Chilko wants. His ears are at attention and his nose is sniffing overtime. I look into the shadows to see what he sees, but I realize what it is too late.

"No!" I shout, swiping at his tail, but he's off — after a skunk.

There's the crash of dog into bush and the *pffsshhht* of skunk letting it go, and then the yelp of a husky in pain. J swears like a trucker and I wish I could rewind the last ten seconds and steer us clear of the park.

The smell wafts over in a thick cloud and makes me feel like throwing up. I've never been this close to skunk spray before — and I guess neither has Chilko. He stumbles out of the bush, pawing his eyes. He whines and coughs. I walk backward and he walks toward me. This is one time I don't want him anywhere near.

Then I notice he's foaming at the mouth. I look around. Will he need a vet? How am I supposed to get him there?

"Whoa. That's not cool," a voice calls behind me.

I spin around.

It's a stocky guy in a yellow hoodie and ripped jeans. "You got tomato juice?" he asks.

I shake my head. "What does that do?" I gag on the words as I inhale more skunk stench. I have to run across the street, toward the guy, to get some fresh air. Chilko wheezes behind me, but stays where he is.

Up close the guy looks familiar. He's got shaggy hair under his hood. He holds his nose but doesn't back away. "My cat got sprayed last year. You gotta wash them with tomato juice. It gets out the smell. Cans and cans of it. You got a bathtub?"

I nod, still not daring to open my mouth and let the skunk air in. I can't figure out where I know him from.

"Maybe you should call someone to help get him home." He points to Chilko, who's pawing his face and trying to puke. "He looks in bad shape."

How did this happen so fast? I went from having the whole night to roam with him to having a skunk-sprayed dog that's not mine, and nowhere to take him.

"I can't go home," I say. "He's . . . can *you* help me?" I stare at the guy, willing him to say yes. Does he go to my school?

He blinks, surprised. "Whoa, man. I'm on my way home. You can't take that dog inside – he'll stink up the whole house."

"So how am I supposed to get him into a bathtub?" I ask.

"I don't know – find an outside one?"

"That's stupid – who has an outside bathtub?" I glare at him. What's wrong with this guy?

He shakes his head. "Look. I gave you some advice. I'm a nice guy. I gotta go home now. Call your mom or something."

"My mom's dead." I watch his eyebrows rise into his shaggy hair. J put that one in my mouth. It works.

"Aw, man. I can get you the tomato juice, but I don't have an outside bathtub, okay?" He glances at Chilko. "Look – he's not wheezing so much. That's good. Maybe he didn't get a direct hit."

"I'm J."

"Mason," he says, slapping my hand. "How old are you, anyway?"

I shrug. "Old enough."

He blinks. "Whatever, man. I work around the corner. Literally." He points and starts walking.

A light comes on in my head. I know where I've seen this guy before.

Ten minutes later I'm standing in the back of Gerry's Corner Store, where Mason works, surrounded by boxes and cans and newspapers, waiting for Mason to find the last can of tomato juice in the store room. He said there were eight and I've loaded seven into grocery bags, but he thinks we'll need all eight, so he's searching for it. I showed him how much money I have — six dollars and seventy-five cents — and he says he'll expect the rest later. At this point I'm happy to give him whatever he wants.

Chilko waits outside by the loading area. He's stopped sneezing and gagging but he's pretty miserable and his eyes are swollen. Mason says the tomato bath will make him more comfortable — and easier to be around.

"Here it is — you got a bucket?" Mason comes out from behind some boxes with the last can.

"I don't have anything. I can't go home with him like this," I say.

"Won't your aunt understand? I mean, there're lots of skunks around here. Dogs and cats get sprayed all the time."

"I don't think so. She's not like that."

"She won't help you in your time of need?"

"You don't know my aunt," I say. I gave Mason the basics about my living situation, but I haven't told him that Chilko isn't my dog. It's best if he knows as little as possible.

He shrugs. "That's too bad. Well, the only thing I can think of is two doors down there's a preschool. They have a plastic kiddie pool that's empty right now, and this morning I saw it on their lawn." He points at me. "I guess you're stealing the kiddie pool."

"Me?"

"Well, I'm in this far enough for my liking," Mason says, holding up his hands. "You can get your hands dirty now."

"Come on, Mason," I say. "I don't want to steal a kiddie pool."

"Man, this is your issue, not mine." He turns away, grabbing a chocolate bar from a box.

"Do you get freebies here?" I ask.

"I don't have to pay for everything right away," he mutters. "They trust me, I *work* here."

I stare at him, wondering how I got into this mess in the first place. Oh yeah — J followed Chilko and Chilko chased a skunk and now we're all here with Mason who'll tell me what to do but won't help. I sit on a box of toilet paper and it sags under me. J has to think quick. "Do the owners check their stock room? I could come back tomorrow and tell them you're stealing their stock."

"Nice try. It's not going to work. Just stop your fear mongering." He chomps the chocolate bar.

"Or you could just help me now, because otherwise I'll stay here all night with my reeking dog, and maybe I'll rub him all over your store. Got enough tomato juice for that?"

"Come on. He's not a biological weapon," Mason says.

"Oh no?" I call Chilko and his big, stinky head appears in the doorway.

Mason groans. "Fine. But you're doing all the work. I'm just lookout."

My stomach grumbles. I take a piece of Mason's chocolate. J feels like some kind of superhero. He thinks in some insane way, this could be fun.

The street is empty and quiet. Most of the apartments are dark.

"It's over there." Mason points.

Beside a purple house with a big preschool sign is a pink and yellow paddling pool. It's empty. It waits for us. My heart starts thumping.

"I'll stay here and let you know if someone comes," Mason says. "Just go and grab it as fast as you can. Speed is the thing here."

"What if I trip?" I ask. The preschool's lawn, separated by a chain-link fence, seems really far away right now.

"You'll be fine," Mason whispers. "Go. Don't trip." He pushes me onto the sidewalk.

A waft of skunk hits my nose. I run.

The paddling pool is the only thing in my vision, so I don't see the guy walking along the sidewalk on the other side of the street until I'm already pulling the pool behind me, gasping for breath.

"Hey!" he shouts. "Pranksters! That's stealing!"

"Mason!" I shout, like he can do something about this. Why didn't he warn me? He was lookout!

Mason's running toward me, swearing. "Sorry J, didn't see him." He grabs the other side of the half-inflated pool and we run around the corner store.

Chilko's still wheezing beside the empty milk crates, and we both hold our breath until we get the pool behind the garage door.

One minute. Two. No knocking, no more shouting. The man must have kept walking.

"You think he'll call the cops?" I ask. It seems like everything that happens to me when I'm out roaming involves the police.

Mason pants and wipes his face. "Nah. He didn't see us come in here."

Since he messed up the whole lookout thing, I don't completely trust Mason's opinion, but we wrestle the pool out the door again and Mason goes to get the can opener.

Chilko does not like being washed with tomato juice.

He stands in the pool without struggling too much, but the whole time I pour juice over him, trying not to gag, he howls. He howls in this moaning way that's like someone died. Mason tries to make him feel better by talking to him about getting dry and not smelling like skunk, but he just keeps howling.

I use the empty can to scoop up more juice and pour it over Chilko's head. He flattens his ears and then shakes all the juice over me and Mason and the back wall of the corner store.

"Hey, man — I've got to clean this up. That's not cool." Mason goes to find a towel.

"Just wait a little longer," I gasp. "Soon you'll stink like tomatoes and not skunk." The smell is still really bad and I have a feeling this isn't working. Maybe we need more juice. Maybe he's supposed to soak in it. I don't think he'll lie down in the pool for a lifetime of dog treats.

Mason comes back with some paper towel and starts wiping the wall down. "He still reeks," he says, coughing.

"I don't think it worked," I say. "What am I going to do?"

"Uh, go home? Confess? So you were out after bedtime — all kids get in trouble at some point." Mason shrugs. "I got my first grounded-for-life when I was thirteen."

"You don't understand — "

I don't get to finish my sentence because right then a car pulls up to the back of the corner store. My heart stops. I drop the can and look for a good exit. Chilko quits howling and shakes again, spraying us. There's no escape. I fly behind a pile of boxes. Mason sees me and grimaces. I send him "I'm not here" messages in my head. I just hope he'll cover for me.

A woman gets out of the car. "Mason Kreeley, what in

blazes are you doing?" she shouts. Her arms fly up as she yells. She wears a dressing gown and a really angry expression.

Mason grabs Chilko's collar, gagging at the stench. "Don't flip out. I was only trying to help," he stutters.

"Oh, you better have a good explanation for this!" The woman stares at the tomato-spattered walls and ground and the kiddie pool and the stinky dog.

"This is Chilko," Mason says. "He needed help."

The woman splutters and waves her arms again. "That's Mrs. Johnson's play pool. Why is it here, with a dog in it?"

Mason winces. "We — I just — he got sprayed by a skunk."

The woman rolls her eyes. "Yeah, I got that much from the odour."

"He was pretty messed up. I had to help."

The woman shakes her head. "Mason, you're too old to smack around, but believe me, if you were younger — "

"Yeah, I've heard it before, Mom," Mason says.

Mom? I shift to see better behind the boxes.

"It's nice of you to help the dog, but really, Mason, you're not usually so thoughtful. Where's the owner?"

"I don't know. He's probably a stray." He holds on as Chilko tries to get out of the pool. "How'd you know I was here?"

"Tom Webber saw you in the preschool yard and called me." Mrs. Kreeley bends to look at Chilko, who's dripping in the pool, looking sad. "This guy's got a really bad dose of skunk. Tomato juice won't do it."

My foot is falling asleep as I crouch behind the boxes, but I don't dare move in case I make a noise.

Mason's mom sighs. "I've got some shampoo at home left from the cat. Tie the dog up and come get it. You can hose him down and then it's up to you." She points a finger at Mason. "I expect all this mess to be gone by morning. Understand?" She glances at something on the floor. "You been snacking again? Remember what happened when Dad found your last pile of wrappers."

Mason follows her to the car without looking at me.

I have no choice but to wait.

Mason comes back with the shampoo but by then I'm starting to panic. It's already 4:09. I didn't expect to be out so late. The sun will be up in less than an hour. It's cold out here too. Chilko's coat keeps him warm even though he's wet, but my hoodie is thin cotton and it's been a long time since dinner. I'm ready to eat something from the store and let Mason take the heat.

"Oh, man, the stink's even worse than before," Mason moans, holding his nose.

"You're so dramatic," I say. "I've been waiting for almost an hour and I haven't passed out from the fumes."

Mason rolls his eyes. "You sound like my mom."

"You got the shampoo?"

"Yup. But you can do the soaping." Mason throws the bottle at me.

I catch it and let Chilko sniff it. He moans a little.

"This isn't your dog, is it?"

I look up from twisting off the cap.

Mason crosses his arms over his chest. "Whose dog is it?"

J can't ignore that one. Mason's my only ally right now. "He's belongs to a friend," I say.

"Uh-huh. Well, your 'friend' must really trust you. You missed behind his ear."

I look down at the foam covering Chilko's neck. At least it's got a smell that helps to take away the skunk stench.

Suddenly I feel like I could sleep for a week. This is so much more than I bargained for tonight. I just want to crawl into bed and forget it ever happened.

Chilko shifts and whines, looking at me.

"You're being really good," I tell him. "Almost done." I soap up his back legs and tail, and soon he looks like a white, fluffy soap-dog.

"Uh — not sure you were supposed to use that much," Mason says. He picks up the bottle, reads the label. "Fifty pounds, is he?"

"I don't know. Probably more." I reach for the hose before Chilko tries to shake. "Just figured I'd cover my bases."

Mason shrugs. "I have no idea where you're from, or if J is your real name. Maybe you're a runaway. But you're pretty attached to that dog. I wish I was that into something."

I turn on the hose and pray Chilko will stay in the kiddie pool. I know I'm going to end up soaking wet either way. The water makes the shampoo drip off in foamy clumps.

"I can't believe he's just staying there," Mason says. "Are you a dog whisperer?"

"A what?"

He steps back as water sprays the wall. "A guy who can train dogs and talk to them, understand them."

"We're just buddies," I say. "We roam together. I think he gets me."

At that moment, Chilko decides he's had enough of the pool and water and shampoo, and leaps out. I'm not close enough to grab his collar. Mason is too slow to grab anything but air.

"Chilko!" I drop the hose and run after him.

He takes off in the direction of the preschool lawn, leaving a white soapy trail on the sidewalk.

Mason and I sprint behind him, but soon it's obvious what he wants.

He wants to roll in the dirt. He chooses a dusty spot, flops on his back and rubs into the ground, wiggling his feet in the air. When he gets up a second later, he's not a white soapy dog anymore.

Mason shoves me in the shoulder. "Nice one."

I shove him back. "It's not *my* fault."

He shoves me again. "Right, like this whole thing isn't your fault. Who took someone else's dog out in the middle of the night?"

I go to shove him back, but he jumps out of reach.

"Admit it — you're in so much crap it's not even funny!" he jeers.

I stare at Chilko, who sniffs around the grass with cedar twigs stuck to his tail. "You're right. I'm in such crap."

Mason chuckles. He snorts when he laughs.

I can't help it — I start cracking up.

Chilko watches us. There's a pine cone stuck to his forehead.

Soon we're on the grass, holding our bellies, Mason snorting like a pig and making me laugh harder. Chilko comes over and sniffs us. There are tiny bubbles on the end of his nose. I wipe them off with my finger.

I help Mason clean up the stock room, but it's starting to get light out as we put the kiddie pool back.

"You'd better get out of here," he says. "I'll put the rest away."

"You sure?" I ask.

"Go. Get home. Maybe I'll get a sainthood for this someday." Mason pulls a mop out of the storage room.

I reach my hand out. It feels right to do it.

He shakes my hand and smiles. "You're all right, J. Come by sometime, bring the dog — during the day."

I grin back, saying I'll try, but of course I can't. Not with Chilko.

"Or give me a call," Mason says. "We could hang out."

This is the first phone number I've programmed into my phone that wasn't a relative or Grant. I can't stop smiling.

After that, Chilko's in a mad rush to get to water — he runs through the park as we head for home, and as soon as he sees the fountain with the rock sculpture in the middle, he heads straight for it. The park is still shadowy and deserted. I glance at the houses around, but no lights are on. It's 4:48. My legs are heavy and move slower than I want them to.

Chilko splashes in the fountain, sticking his nose under and shaking his whole body. I throw water over his back to get rid of the last of the shampoo and dirt, but at this point I don't care. I just want to get home.

When Chilko is as clean as he's going to get, I start walking away toward the street that leads to my house. He'll get the picture. I pull out my phone to check Mason's number one more time. Chilko's still jumping around in the fountain.

"Idiot dog," I mutter, but it makes me smile. I snap a photo. Evidence of this crazy night I can send to Grant. In the end I have to call Chilko, but when I do he comes sprinting over, his ears pressed against his head. He rips past me, spraying water from his tail. We walk the rest of the way quickly. It's 5:07 and a couple of cars have passed us. Aunt Laura will be home in a few hours. How on earth am I going to act like I slept all night?

On the corner of Sixth and Chesterfield, Chilko wants to head up the hill, but I need to turn left to my house. I take that as the place we have to part. He must live up there somewhere. I kneel beside him, braving the smell, and put my hand on his neck. He leans into me a little, and I don't even mind that my pants will be stained.

I point down my street. "Time to go home."

He looks at me seriously. There's a spot of crusty white foam on his forehead.

There's no way I'll see him again. His owner will know he got out and was sprayed by a skunk and now he'll keep him inside at night. I don't even know where he lives. Suddenly the world seems like such an unfair place where everyone I care about ends up leaving. I shiver, pulling my hood up.

Chilko turns and trots away up the hill. I watch him go.

A wave of tiredness drops onto me, and as I turn to keep walking, a car drives up and stops. I freeze.

"Hey, aren't you Laura's nephew?" a woman's voice asks.

I try to turn my face away. "No, I'm — "

"Jakob! That's you, isn't it?"

Crap. I turn back, trying to think of a good excuse. Why hasn't J made one up, ready to use?

"It's awfully early to be out, isn't it?" the woman says. She looks sort of familiar — maybe she lives down the street.

"I was — looking at the stars," I mumble. "I wanted to find some constellations."

The woman frowns. "Well, most stars are gone now. You should try midnight, not six in the morning."

"Yeah, you're right," I say. "I'll try that next time."

I back away and give a little wave. "Bye!"

The woman drives slowly beside me. "Where's your aunt, Jakob?"

I pause. "At work." No point in lying. I know Aunt Laura will hear from this lady by noon today.

"So you're home alone?"

"No, we have tenants downstairs." I keep walking, hoping the woman will give up.

"Well, it would be a real shame if you're getting into trouble," she says.

"I'm not in trouble," I say quickly. "I just walked to the park to look at the stars."

The woman raises her eyebrows. "Then why are your clothes so dirty?"

CHAPTER 7

I wake up to Aunt Laura's footsteps in the hall. My head feels fuzzy and like it's made of lead. My eyelids are glued shut. Every noise — ticking clock, creaking floor — sounds so *loud*. I burrow deeper into the covers, but then I remember: my clothes are in the washing machine. I fell asleep before I could put them into the dryer. I sit up, rubbing my eyes so they'll open.

I have two choices. Get up now and tell Aunt Laura about the woman in the car, so she hears it from me first. Keep to my "looking at the stars" story. Claim my clothes weren't messy. Choice number two: go back to sleep and deny everything when it comes up.

I pull the covers over my head.

"Jakob?"

"Mrph," I answer from under my pillow.

"Jakob, it's noon. Are you sick?"

"Nuh."

A hand touches my shoulder. "Do you have a fever?"

I can't put it off any longer. I turn over. My room is baking hot — the curtains are open and sun streams in. My pyjamas are soaked. Maybe I do have a fever — or feel like I do to Aunt Laura. I decide to play that angle.

She sits beside me and feels my forehead. "It's roasting in

here. And why does it smell like skunk?"

"I don't feel good," I say. "My stomach is upset."

She wrinkles her forehead. "Do you feel achy?"

I nod.

"Why would Mrs. Lester leave a message on the machine about you being out at night? She said she saw you wandering the streets at six this morning."

Crap. I consider choice number one again.

"I was reading one of Dad's star books," I say slowly. "I wanted to see Ursa Major, so I went to the park. I was only gone a little while."

Aunt Laura narrows her eyes at me. "But why did you have to leave the house? And why did Mrs. Lester say your clothes were filthy? Were you rolling around in the dirt or something?"

I gulp. My throat is completely dry. "I need some water," I croak.

She reaches for the glass on my dresser.

"I wanted to get away from the lights," I say, making it up as I go. "Dad said stars are easier to see without light pollution, and I thought the park — " I groan and hold my head.

Aunt Laura looks half sceptical, half believing. She stares at me for a long time. "You're too young to be out like that. I don't want to see you in Emerg — or worse."

I nod. "I know. Sorry."

She gets up. "I can make you some broth for your stomach."

I turn over and face the wall. I'll have to keep up the sick act all day, but in reality I could eat three meals at once.

Once Aunt Laura's out running errands, I eat two huge bowls of cereal and sneak out of the house without seeing Libby, although I keep looking over my shoulder until I get three streets away, just in case — I can never be too careful with her. It has to be the hottest day of summer so far and in minutes my back and neck are sweating. Kids with bikes and skateboards stream in and out of Gerry's Corner Store with slushies and candy. I stand across the street for a moment, watching. I was here just hours ago and everything looked so different — *was* so different. I feel for the change in my pocket. Just enough to cover what I owe him.

Inside the store it's much cooler, which must be why there are kids and a few adults hanging out in the aisles, obviously not buying anything. Mason's behind the counter looking about as tired as I feel. He has a bad case of bed head.

I get in line behind a girl with giant slushies in each hand. Normally the sight would make me want to buy one, but today the cups overflowing with neon pink and green make me feel sick. I guess my mom would be happy about that — she could never understand how Grant and I could throw back a giant slushie every day. *It'll make your insides bright pink*, she'd say. *Mmm, pink insides*, I'd reply, slurping from my straw, and Grant would laugh.

"J — what are you doing here?"

I'm suddenly at the front of the line. Mason blinks at me tiredly. "I came to pay you back," I say.

He looks surprised. "Oh, yeah. Thanks. Hey, I'm going for a sanity break now." He looks over his shoulder. "Want to meet me around back?"

I wait beside the double doors into the stock room feeling a little like someone with a backstage pass at a concert — only there are no famous bands or crazy parties.

Right now I'm just a little cooler than the kids in the candy aisle. There's still skunk stink hanging around, but no one would guess what happened last night.

One of the doors opens and Mason pops his head out. "I didn't mean you had to pay me back within twenty-four hours or anything. I mean, it's cool that you're here, but — " He looks around, motioning me inside.

The stockroom is even colder than the front of the store. I could hang out here all day. "I was just walking by and I had the money," I lie.

He grins. "That was a crazy night, man. My mom was super-suspicious — she still thinks something fishy happened here."

"Or something skunky."

"Exactly."

"Well, it did," I say, pulling out the change.

"So did Chilko get home okay?" Mason drops the coins into his back pocket without counting them.

I stare at a huge box that says Doritos on the side. "I guess so."

"You guess so? Don't you know where he lives?" Mason stares at me a little too hard.

"Yeah, of course," I say. "I just mean he was still pretty messed up from the skunking. It was rough."

"Tell me about it. My mom's making me work here for the next five days with no time off. I have a summer to live, you know?" Mason kicks the leg of a metal rack but it doesn't budge. From the look on his face I can tell he hurt his toe.

"Yeah, I know. So, do you skate?" I ask.

Mason shakes his head. "I ride. You?"

"Like, mountain biking?"

"Yup." He takes it from my question that I don't. "The

North Shore has the best riding in the world. Lots of technical trails and crazy stunts. You've got to take advantage of that. Do you have a bike?"

"Yeah, but it's — "

"You should come with me sometime. You'd need full-suspension, though. I could get my buddy's bike for you to borrow. I'll take it easy on you, of course." He swings his arm to slap my shoulder.

"Uh, yeah. That'd be great," I say, even though the thought of mountain biking with Mason, who could be semi-pro for all I know, kind of scares me. But the idea of hanging out with him doesn't. "When do you usually go?"

"Oh, every day when I'm not here." He scowls at the boxes and cans around us. "And sometimes after work too." He looks at me. "I bet you'd be a good rider. You're pretty fearless, right?"

"Hey, Mason — where're the rolls of pennies?" A guy pokes his head around the doorway. "We're kind of slammed here."

"Ugh. I'll have to get them," Mason grumbles, rolling his eyes at me. "Talk to you later, J?"

It's not until I'm walking home, sweating bullets again, that I really get what happened back there. I have a new friend. It was pretty easy too — except for the whole skunk night. Who knows what will happen, but at least I'm a little less alone now.

The rest of the day goes by so easy it's like time is sped up. I actually find something decent to watch on TV while I pretend to be sick. Aunt Laura brings me more soup and lemonade. I daydream about riding the trails with Mason.

---

j, i had the most awesome time with johannes. it's like he's you but german. he's only been skating for a few months, but we did some pretty hard tricks. if you ever come to visit, we could all hang out. i don't really know what sirius is. wasn't he in harry potter?

My alarm jolts me out of sleep at 11:50 pm, but then I remember. It's stupid to even wait for Chilko. His owners will have seen his filthy, skunk-infused coat and kept him in their yard or inside. There's no way he'll be roaming around tonight.

But what if he does show up? My backpack is ready to go. I've got the map. I could go alone. I lie back in bed. Yeah, I could go alone. I haven't thought about that before. The idea of wandering around looking for someplace I can't even describe seems way crazier if I don't have Chilko with me.

I pull out the map and turn on my bedside light. Maybe if I can find another street name that triggers something. I stare at the little roads and parks until my vision gets blurry.

I wake up with the map over my face, but that wasn't what woke me. There's a sound coming from the living room. I open the door, needing to pee anyway, but before I get there I realize what the sound is. I peek around the wall.

The TV's on but muted. She sits on the couch with her back to me. Her shoulders are hunched and every so often they shudder. She sniffs.

I back away, sliding my feet on the floor, praying there are no creaks.

"Jakob?"

I close my door silently and listen. No footsteps. I walk

over and open my window. This isn't the first time I've peed on the bushes outside my room. Then I turn off my light, lie down and throw my blanket over my head.

Try not to think of her sitting out there. Stare at the dark and breathe.

The next morning there's a note from Aunt Laura beside the box of cereal on the table. She's got an appointment, back by noon. Says she'll take Libby and me to the beach.

I pour cereal into a bowl and then add milk, watching as the cereal escapes over the edge. If I eat slow enough, maybe I won't have to deal with Libby until Aunt Laura gets back. I'm feeling bad about the drawing she did of me and if I see her I might say something stupid, like "I'm sorry."

But after three bites, there's a knock on the back door. Libby's face peers in through the window. Because she's pulled her hair back really tight, her forehead looks huge.

"I've been reading about Carmen Rosemont's nature series. I need to draw fish," she says after letting herself in. A pencil is already in her hand.

I'm not sure how to take her randomness. And though I know she wants me to, I do *not* want to ask who this Carmen Rosemont is. I keep shoving cereal into my mouth.

"What kind of cereal is that?"

"I don't know. Something healthy. Go to the Aquarium. Lots of fish there." I fill my mouth so I can't talk anymore.

"Carmen says you have to be in the real world, the true, harsh world, to really get the experience on the paper. I want natural habitat. Mom said you know where all the rivers and streams are around here."

I shrug. Thanks, Soleil.

"Will you show me? I'm all ready to go."

I glance at the clock. Three hours until Aunt Laura gets home. I don't know why, but I find myself saying yes.

After tapping the table with the eraser end of her pencil and grinning at me, she sort of flies out of the kitchen and I turn back to my cereal, wondering why I was feeling so guilty before.

"Is there another creek? This one doesn't have any fish," Libby says as we pick our way along the crusty, muddy stream bed. It's July. What did she expect?

There's MacKay Creek, but I really don't feel like walking another half an hour for some stupid fish. "This is it," I say.

She squats beside a rock covered in dry moss. "I guess I can sketch some plants. I really wanted fish."

"Doesn't Carmen talk about flexibility?" I mutter.

"Huh?" She's busy peering into the middle of a giant fern.

"Never mind. What about birds?" I say as a robin hops along the trail a few metres away.

"Birds are good," she murmurs, her eyes on the robin, following the way it moves. Without taking her eyes from it, she opens her sketchbook, grabs a pencil and starts making lines.

The robin hops under a salmonberry bush. Its tail goes up and down as it looks for food.

"See those white and black speckles around his eyes?" Libby says quietly.

"Yeah?" I squat down.

"Aren't they beautiful?"

I wouldn't call them beautiful, but I don't say that. The robin comes back onto the trail, something in his beak. He tilts his head, pauses, then flies up into a tree.

"Got him," Libby says.

"You're done? That was, like, ten seconds." I walk over to where she's sitting and look over her shoulder.

At first it looks like scratchy lines and shadows, but as I look closer I can see his tail, the fan-shape and the way it moved as he leaned forward to pick something up. It's not really a bird she's drawn, but since I was there, since I saw him, I can see him on the page.

"How did you do that?" I ask.

"It's just drawing the story. Like you said, ten seconds. Carmen does this to warm up before she works on a new project. Some of her sketches are in her exhibitions. There's this really amazing one of a turtle . . ." She turns the page of her sketchbook over. "You want to try?"

I stand up. "No thanks. Drawing's not my thing."

"It's not about being good. It's about looking for the story."

"I'm not good at stories either."

Libby gets up, holding out her sketchbook. "That's not true."

"Look, you don't know me."

"I don't need to know you. Everyone knows stories. Everyone can see things happen. Just draw it." She holds out the book. Her eyes are way too serious. I can imagine how creeped out the art camp kids were.

"I'm just the tour guide here." I hold up my hands.

"Carmen says — "

"I don't care what Carmen says," I snap. I don't really want to know, but the look on Libby's face — like she's been slapped — makes me feel bad. "So who is Carmen Rosemont anyway?" I hate that I feel bad. "Was she your art teacher?"

Libby shakes her head, looking at her knee.

"Really — tell me," I say.

"She's an artist in New York. She's had exhibitions all over the world — she's really famous. And she's a feminist."

"Great."

"Haven't you ever been passionate about something?"

"No," I say, but I don't even sound convincing to me.

"Isn't there anything you're so into you can't stop thinking about it and you want to live it all day, every day?" She doodles on the new page of her sketchbook without looking at it.

"Yeah, I guess. Maybe." I lean against a tree trunk. But I screwed up my thing and I'll never see it again.

"Well, then you understand. I love to draw." She holds out the pencil and book again. "Come on. You won't look stupid, I promise."

Knowing this could be the lamest thing I've ever done, I take the book and the pencil.

"Now just choose something to draw. Anything." She looks around. "How about that tree?"

I follow her finger. "The one with all the crazy branches?"

"Sure. It looks angry, don't you think?"

I hold out her stuff. "Show me first. You're better at it."

"No, I'm not. You haven't even tried yet."

"Libby, this is stupid." I feel even more stupid holding her stuff because she won't take it back.

"Why? Because you might not like what you draw? Who cares? Who says it has to look a certain way?"

"I just can't do it." I reach down to put the sketchbook on the ground.

"Wait — draw this leaf." She holds out a salmonberry branch. "Sit right there and draw what your hand sees."

"And where's the story there?" I ask, the sketchbook heavy in my arm.

She smiles, holds the leaf out. "It's in whatever you draw."

The whole time I'm drawing the leaf, J screams in my head about stupid artsy crap and how idiotic this all is. She is nuts. I'm nuts too.

It takes about two minutes of scratching on the page before my dark blob looks anything like the leaf. But it actually kind of does. J grumbles, but before he can start up again, Libby steps in front of me.

"See? You did great. It's totally a leaf. Now try this flower."

"Thanks, but I think it's your turn again," I say, handing back her sketchbook. "My hand's tired."

She shrugs and squats in front of the blue flower, already drawing. "You have to draw more, Jakob. You should practise."

"What am I practising for? It's not a sport."

"I'll draw one, then you draw one."

J complains loudly that this will seriously kill the rest of the morning. "I think we should get back to the house," I say. "My aunt's going to be home soon."

"You don't have to be scared," she says.

I want to shake her. "I'm *not* scared."

"Fine. You're not scared."

I pull off a salmonberry leaf and shred it. "I'm not."

She watches the pieces fall to the ground. "I know. It's obvious."

"What is?"

"That you're not scared."

I throw up my hands. "Man — are you like this with your friends?"

She goes back to her drawing.

On our way home from the creek, Libby starts going on about feminism and pop art as if I'm actually interested.

I try to smile and nod, but after a while I can feel a headache coming on. I just want to get home, so I suggest we take a short cut.

"That's where my mom's new boyfriend lives." She points down the street. "The blue house with the brown roof."

"What's he like?" I ask, not really caring, but happy that a question has made her stop the art lecture.

"He's really nice. He has this cool dog. We took it for a walk yesterday."

My stomach tightens, even though it could be any guy and any dog. What are the chances? J says the chances are pretty good. We're only three streets up from my house.

"What kind of dog?" I ask, my heart already hammering in my chest.

Libby walks down the lane. "Come on. I'll show you."

She stops in front of a chain-link fence. I try to breathe normally as I come up beside her. The grass stretches from the fence to the back of the blue house. On the lawn are dog toys — bones and ropes and balls. Inside a big cardboard box, the kind used for fridges or stoves, is a black and white dog. He lies on his side, asleep.

"His name's Chilko," Libby's saying. "He's huge but Patrick says he's not dangerous. Big dogs freak me out sometimes, but Chilko seems nice. Do you want to meet him?"

His name's Chilko. His owner's name is Patrick. Patrick's dating Soleil.

My life just got more complicated in a million ways.

"Uh — no," I say. "I'm not a dog person. I like cats better." J keeps feeding me lies, but I clamp my mouth shut.

Libby looks at me. "Are you sure? He's not a mean dog."

"I just don't like dogs that much."

Footsteps crunch behind us. I freeze.

Libby turns around with a smile. "Oh, hi, George."

A skinny blond guy is standing there. He looks too old for the skater T-shirt and jeans he's wearing.

"Hi," George says. "Libby, right?"

"Yeah, and this is — "

"I'm J," I say, putting my hands in my pockets.

"Are you here to walk Chilko?" Libby asks.

George opens the gate and nods. "Yup. You guys want to come in?"

I say no at the same time Libby says yes.

George blinks. "Whatever. I'm just going to get his leash." He walks across the lawn, whistling to Chilko. I wish I'd thought of doing that when we were out at night. Chilko springs up when he hears the whistle and comes bounding over to George. His tail makes a circle behind him.

"Are you nervous?" Libby asks, touching my hand that grips the chain-link fence.

I pull away. "Why would I be nervous? I just think we should go."

But Chilko's seen us. His ears are up. His eyes lock onto mine. It takes him two seconds to cover the distance between us.

He almost knocks me over with his paws and Libby jumps back. It's her turn to look scared.

"Whoa, he really likes you," she says. "I only saw him act like that with Patrick."

I don't meet her gaze.

Chilko's wagging his tail for me, sniffing my clothes and turning around so I can scratch his back. He moans a little in his wolfy way. I bury my fingers in his fur, feeling like I haven't seen him in a year. And how great it would be if I could walk him in daylight.

"You make him crazy," George says, walking up with the leash. "Do you know huskies?"

"No," I say, stepping back. "He just ran over."

I can feel Libby's eyes on me, but I can't look at her. I'm glued to Chilko. He's acting like all his favourite people are here. I've never seen him so happy. At night he acts more quiet and aloof.

"We better get going, buddy," George says. "You guys want to come?"

"Well," Libby begins.

"We can't," I finish for her. "We have to get home."

"Sure. Nice to meet you, Jake," George says.

"It's J," I say.

"Right, J. See you around." He leads Chilko out of the yard and up the alley.

"Bye, Chilko," Libby says quietly beside me.

As we walk across the next street, I try to find the right words. I know she's suspicious. She hasn't said anything, and that's unusual.

"I guess I'm a dog whisperer or something," I mumble. Right after, I wish I hadn't listened to J on that one. I want to tell her the truth or ask her if she knows, but even I know that's the stupidest thing I could do.

We walk into the next alley, past a fence with a yapping dachshund that waddles along beside us, protecting his yard.

"There was a story in all that, wasn't there?" Libby says.

"What are you talking about?" I ask too quickly.

She stares ahead, as if trying to see something far away. "The way he greeted you. His wagging tail. It was pure happiness. I'd love to draw that."

Getting home is a blur because of all the new complications floating around in my head. Aunt Laura actually keeps her promise and takes Libby and me to the beach, but I can't do anything but lie in the sand and think. It doesn't even feel like thinking — it's bouncing from one problem, one lie, to another. I can't count how many I've told so far. It's a pretty big number.

My mom always knew when I was lying. It was some kind of superpower, like she could see inside me and find the lie circling around in my bloodstream. When I was five I lied about taking cookies from the package we were saving for a party. She stared me down until I started blubbing and confessed, in tears. From that day on, I couldn't lie to her. Her power was too strong. But now that she's not here, I can lie any time I want and get away with it. Part of me feels free when I lie, but another part gets a little more trapped.

Libby wades in the water with a bucket, looking for crabs. Seagulls fly above her. Aunt Laura leans against a log and reads a magazine about the broken marriages of movie stars. It could be a scene from a perfect afternoon. Any stranger seeing us would think so. Only I know the truth.

I must have dozed off because next thing I know, Libby's shaking my foot.

"What?"

"Time to turn over," she says. Her head blocks the sun and for a second it's like she's surrounded by a halo.

I must be losing it. "What?" I ask again.

"You're burning. Time to do the other side." She points at my legs, which are getting pretty lobsterish below my shorts. Aunt Laura offered me sunscreen but I was too lazy to put it on.

"Or you could come help me with the crabs," Libby says.

"What?" I glance over at Aunt Laura but she's asleep under the tent of her magazine.

"You say 'what' a lot."

"Well, you're kind of random."

She kneels beside me, holding out a crab in her palm.

I sit up, worried she'll drop it down my shirt or something, but that would be what Grant would do.

"I caught a bunch in a bucket and now I'm going to — "

"Let me guess. You're going to draw them."

She rolls her eyes. "No. I was going to make a race track for them. Didn't you ever have crab races when you were a kid?"

So we end up making an oval Formula One track in the sand, shored up with rocks and more sand and with a round hill in the middle to discourage the crabs from getting off course.

I haven't played like this at the beach for a long time — probably since my parents took me when I was a kid. We'd make huge sandcastles. The bigger the better. Dad and I were the builders and Mom was the decorator. She searched the beach for small black pebbles or white shells while we put up the walls and towers and drawbridge. When it was finished, I'd put a stick through the top as a flagpole and we'd eat lunch and watch the sea come in and wash the foundation away.

Libby stands back from the oval track and smiles at me. "I think it's ready."

"Wait." I get on my knees and reach over the track's short wall. I trace a line with my finger in the sand. "We need a starting line. Right?"

"Great. Now, how many should be in the first heat?"

"Heat? Is this the Olympics?"

Libby looks at me like I'm an idiot. "I have done this before. Trust me. We'll have to do a few heats. If we put them all on the track, it'll be a free-for-all and a big mess."

"Of course. Stupid me."

"So, I say we start with five." She reaches into the bucket.

"Do you want to make lanes too? And we could put little numbers on their backs."

"Don't take it so seriously, Jakob. It's just fun."

I stare at her with my mouth open. "Uh, yeah. Was that not clear from my sarcasm?"

She fake-flings a crab at me, making the same open-mouthed face I did. "Uh, yeah, Jakob. Didn't you know I could be sarcastic too?"

I don't really know what to say to that, so I reach into her bucket and pull out the biggest crab, which pinches me on the finger. He drops into the track and scuttles along the base of the hill.

"Head start — no fair," Libby says. "We need to choose five and start them together."

"Fine. You do it." I squat beside the track and fold my arms across my knees.

"I can see you haven't done this before," she says again, reaching into the bucket with both hands and bringing out four crabs.

"And you're some kind of expert crab racer?"

She puts the crabs near the starting line, grabs a stick and sweeps them all in the same direction. For a moment, it works. They all skitter away from the stick. Then a couple decide they want to go backwards and two more attack each other. "I used to do this with my dad," she says.

"I didn't even know you had one," I say. "Does he live here?"

"Calgary," she says.

"So you don't see him much?"

She shakes her head, eyes on the crabs, which she's still poking forward with the stick. One is actually making progress around the track. My big one is almost at the top of the hill, waving a claw around.

"What's he like?" I'm not sure why I'm asking. Maybe because I'd never thought about Libby having a dad, or Soleil having an ex-husband.

She shrugs. "He has the same colour hair as me. He plays guitar in a band. He has a new family, though. He got married two years ago and had a baby."

"Have you seen them?"

"Once. The baby was kind of cute, but he drooled everywhere."

For someone who wouldn't shut up the past few days, she isn't saying much now. "Does he know about your art?" I ask, thinking this might be something she'll get more excited about.

The first crab makes it back to the starting line, thanks to Libby's prodding. She picks it up and puts it in the bucket.

"You should send him some," I say. "I bet he'd like to see what you've been drawing."

"I have," she says. "Twice. And he didn't say anything."

"Maybe he didn't get them," I say, even though it's stupid. I'm not sure why I'm doing this.

She plucks my big crab off the hill and puts him at the starting line. "He got them. He sent me some pencils to use. Only they were the wrong ones. He used to call me Creative Girl, like I was a superhero or something. It seems pretty stupid now."

"No, it doesn't," I lie.

Libby straightens her legs and picks up the bucket. "I'm going to put these guys back."

"But that was only one heat."

"It's not working. It never worked. Dad used to make these funny commentator voices, but — never mind. I'm ready to go anyway."

I sit beside the track, watching my big crab hike the hill again. By our log, Aunt Laura is packing up her stuff.

CHAPTER 8

---

i found the AWESOMEST place for skating, j. kicks the butt of anything we used to try. johannes and i go there almost every day — you'd be so stoked too. hope you can see it someday :)

Mom and Dad are in the living room looking through his telescope. It points out the window but the sun shines in. No way are they seeing any stars. I wonder for a second if they're spying on someone, but the telescope is too powerful for that — it's for things thousands of miles away. Come take a look, Jakob, *Mom says when she sees me.* What is it? *I ask, worried it's not something I want to see.* Just come and look, *Dad says. He waves me over, smiling. I just want to hug him, stand next to him and feel his hand on my shoulder, but they're both so into the telescope that I can't stop myself from leaning in and looking into the eye piece.* It's amazing what this beauty can show us, *Dad says. He pats the scope as I squint into the yellow light of a hundred stars. It's beautiful, but it doesn't make sense — it's not nighttime. I straighten up to tell him this, but they're gone — the room, the house, is gone. I'm back on a dark street that shines with rain. I start jogging, then running. A strange feeling creeps up the back of my neck. Just around another corner, another street. It's so close, I know it. I hear the heartbeat of the car, smell dirt. Someone sobbing.*

The Cosmic Turkeys scream "Bite Me" in my ear. I pull out my headphones and sit up. A question is fading from my brain. This time I almost got close enough to think it. I'm so close to remembering, I can taste it.

I grab my backpack, stuff in the map. Fence or not, I have to take Chilko with me. This is the only way.

I make it out of the house without waking Aunt Laura, and judging by the darkness in the suite, without waking Soleil and Libby. I feel like an experienced burglar sneaking around with black clothes, tying my laces in front of the hedge, hidden from the road. The night is mine again.

The walk to Chilko's house seems to take seconds. I stand in the street looking at the lights on in the blue house. Patrick lives in the bottom suite, like Soleil. None of the lights are on down there. I can just make out the grey shape of Chilko in the dark. I can't use my flashlight or someone might think I'm breaking in. I wait, try to breathe normally, wait for J to find the guts to make a move.

A cat screeches behind me and I jump into the fence, which makes a *ching* sound and wavers a little. I scramble for cover, diving behind a blackberry bush. Thorns rip into my hands and neck. I don't care. It's hard to hear anything because my heart thuds in my ears.

A minute passes. No more cat, no shouts or footsteps. No doors opening. I take three deep breaths. Inch closer to the fence. The same two lights are on upstairs. I crawl along the fence a few feet. Something snuffles around.

I look up and Chilko's wet nose is sticking through the chain-link. His eyes shine in the dark, looking into mine. His tail wags silently. I'm so relieved he knows it's me that I almost want to stay where I am all night. Just lie here with him and then go home. Wouldn't that be enough?

But J points out that I'm so close. Chilko wants to come with me. He's been waiting.

After another minute, he sits down on his side of the fence. I put my hand through and pet his soft ears. When I get up slowly, careful to make as little sound on the gravel as possible, Chilko follows. He's good at being silent. Suddenly he stops, as if he's been pulled back. He has — he's on a rope. I guess that's what's stopped him from getting out.

I ease the latch back and open the gate. Luckily it doesn't make a noise. I sneak over the concrete path and onto the grass. Chilko waits at the end of his rope. His face says, *We're going roaming, right?* He wasn't this excited to see George. I unclip the rope from his collar, glancing at the house one last time.

This is the moment where I can't turn back. I'm stealing a dog. Not just meeting him on the street at night. I'm taking him from his yard. From now on, I'm a thief. But a friend too, J says. We look out for each other.

My fingers tremble as the rope falls onto the grass. These aren't hands I know. I've turned into a stranger. Who knows what I'll do next?

A light comes on in the basement suite. Before I can think any more, I'm flying out of the gate, closing it behind me, Chilko already in front, running down the alley with his tail high.

I glance back and the light is gone. Maybe I imagined it. Maybe it was J playing with my brain, making me leave the yard. Because he knew if he didn't do something, I was going to bail on the whole plan.

We're on a mission this time and Chilko knows it. It's a relief to be out in the night and roaming, but there's an itch I can't scratch. We're going somewhere, getting closer, but where? Canis Major and Cygnus shine above us. At least they're always there, now that I know how to find them on my own.

By twelve-thirty we're far from home, east of the farthest park I've walked to from my house. The houses are big and old but every once in a while, what Aunt Laura calls a Messy Hippie House pops up. They're easy to recognize because they have lots of plants in the windows and strings of Christmas lights inside all year. I watch to make sure Chilko doesn't go into any yards. Not because hippies aren't friendly, but because I don't need any trouble tonight. No distractions.

I pull out the map as we walk. Each block takes us farther east from Cygnet Street, in the direction of the highway. You have to take the highway to get to the airport, and that's where we were going that night. I read the street names over and over. None of them sounds familiar. We walk on.

In the next block the street goes down a steep hill. The river's not far away — I can hear it. Up ahead there's a park along the river. Lots of dog walkers take their dogs there.

We stop at the corner. Something starts nudging my brain. I look around — there's nothing different about these houses, except for the broken-down car in the front yard of the closest hippie place. This isn't the spot, but it could be close . . .

Chilko noses around in a bush. I whistle and he trots over. I've never thought about bringing a leash for him, but right now I feel the need to have him close. I don't know why. I touch my fingers to his back and he leans into me for a second.

We walk to the next intersection, which is with a main road. A car whips past. Chilko stops at the edge of the sidewalk but I grab his collar anyway. Something's got me by the collar too. It's the twitchy-spine feeling, stronger now, making me want to leave and stay at the same time. I glance at the street sign: Keith Road and Lynnmouth Avenue. A car speeds past, sprays water from its windshield, even though it hasn't rained in weeks. Drops hit my face. As it drives away, I see the glass cleaner spray up, windshield wipers thudding back and forth. The sound is loud in my ears even though the car is long gone: the steady beat in the upside down car, seat belt holding in my breath.

My brain switches off, turns on again, and I'm there. Everything is wet and sticky and dark. Someone moans. I can't tell if it's me or not.

Something brushes my hand, something soft. Fur. A car honks, brakes squeal. I look up and I'm in the middle of the intersection. It's a dark, warm night, stuffy air in my throat. Chilko's beside me, waiting for my next move, but I can't seem to make my legs take a step.

"You need help, kid?" The driver of a blue truck calls behind us. He's a couple of metres away, headlights shining in my face.

I shake my head. My voice doesn't work.

"Then could you get out of the road?"

My hand finds Chilko's fur. He moves forward and somehow I follow. We make it to the other side and the cars drive on behind us.

I lean into a scraggly hedge that itches my neck. This is it. Was it. The accident happened here. It's just a street like the others. No one would ever know.

My knees wobble under me. I thought I'd feel lighter, happier, finally able to breathe, but I just feel . . . more unsure. What happened here? J asks. Why did he crash the car? He always said keep it between the ditches, but he couldn't. Why not? From inside my head, a memory whispers, *Because of you.*

I know I'm a part of this — how the accident happened and why — but it's just not coming back. I shake my head. Chilko stares at me. There's something familiar about him being here too — but that's crazy. He just moved to town. Come on — remember! But what if I don't want to know? What if it's too hard to think about . . .

I pick up a rock and throw it into the street. Chilko bounds after it and I have to call him back. "Let's go," I say as he reaches me. "This is crazy. I'm crazy." I just want to go home.

Before I thought I'd get answers to all my questions, but now I have a million more. They beat against the inside of my skull, making it pound. I just want to forget again. At least forgetting was easier. Dr. Tang said something about that while I was sitting in his overstuffed armchair, trying to answer his questions about the accident. He said maybe my subconscious didn't want to remember because it hurt too much.

Chilko trots ahead as we retrace our route. Pretty soon I'm jogging to keep up. The farther away I get from the intersection, the more split apart I am. I want to be home, in bed, away from all the stupid stuff I can't figure out. But J won't leave me alone. He nags at me, pushing questions, until I hold my head and yell, "Shut up, just shut the hell up!"

Chilko stares at me in midstep. He looks so calm, like yelling at the voices in your head is a normal thing to do. I pull out my dad's star chart. By focusing on the names and shapes of the constellations, I manage to keep J out of my thoughts all the way home.

A hand shakes me awake. My room is boiling hot again. I turn over to look at my clock, but first I see Aunt Laura. She's not in scrubs for once, or pyjamas. She's wearing normal summer clothes and her hair is actually washed.

I feel like I ran a marathon last night — with my body and brain. I croak so she can hear how dry my throat is.

"What's with you these days, Jakob?" she asks. Her voice has actual concern in it. "Are you going through adolescence all at once?"

I mumble that I'm just tired.

"Well, I want us to do something today. All of us."

"All?"

"Libby too." She looks at me hard. "I'm sure she'd like the company."

"But why do you and I suddenly have to hang out together?" I lie back and stare at the peeling paint spots on the ceiling. She still hasn't noticed them.

"What do you mean, 'why'? Because you're my nephew and we should do more than pass each other in the hall. And by the way, we should talk about painting in here, now that you've taken down those old stars. It'll look much cleaner."

I pretend I didn't hear that. "You're wearing normal clothes."

"Right. Normal clothes."

"Why?"

She stares at me, trying to read my face. "I went to talk to someone."

"And?"

She looks around the room. "It's complicated. I'm trying to sort out a lot of stuff right now."

I almost don't say it, but something has to fill the silence. "Is it about the accident?"

She glances at me, then away. "In part. Mostly it's me."

J rises up from where he's been hiding and I say, "Do you feel like you're stuck with me?"

"No, Jakob. Not at all." She goes to put a hand on my knee but stops. "Has something happened? Are you having nightmares?" She always changes the subject when it gets too close.

I throw my legs over the edge of the bed. "No."

Her face relaxes a little. "Listen, we need to get you some summer clothes. You're growing out of most of your jeans."

I know what she's doing. I've been doing it too. We've been living for six months this way. She'll feel better if she buys me things, acts like the guardian she has to be.

"Whatever," I say. "I need to get dressed."

"I'll make you some toast," she says, heading for the door. "Then we can talk about it."

Talk about it. I guess I might win the most lies medal, but Aunt Laura wins the avoiding the elephant in the room medal, hands down.

The phone rings differently in England. For a second I think I've dialled wrong. Then someone picks up and I know that voice.

"Hi, Mrs. Branford. Is Grant there?" It feels weird that she's not in Grant's old house, five minutes away. Did I get the time difference right? I wonder if this is a bad idea.

"Jakob? My goodness. It's good to hear from you." The line crackles a little.

"I just wondered if Grant was home."

"Oh, you just missed him. He's gone out for a few hours. He'll be really sorry he wasn't here. Can he call you back later?"

"Yeah, sure."

"How are you, Jakob?"

"Fine." I try not to sound disappointed but don't think it works.

"How's your aunt?"

"Good. She's — good."

"I'm glad," Grant's mom says. "I know the past while's been hard for you. Grant told us you're getting into astronomy like your dad."

"Uh, well, sort of."

"That's great, Jakob. I think it's so important to do that. Keep those memories close to you. You're a strong guy."

There's a pause and I realize it's my turn.

"Jakob?"

"Yeah. Thanks. I guess I'll talk to Grant later."

Someone says something in the background. "Okay. You take care," Mrs. Branford says.

I press *end* and let the phone drop to the carpet.

I'm in a really bad mood before we even leave for the mall. I've always hated shopping anyway, except when I was little and my mom took me Christmas shopping. She used to take me at the beginning of December so we could avoid the worst lineups. She'd pack us snacks and water in case we didn't get home for a while, and then we'd treat it like a mission: find everyone's presents, buy them, get home before bedtime. She'd make me her sidekick. I was responsible for checking prices. If the salad bowl at Sears was cheaper than the one at Charlie's Kitchen Supplies, we'd race back to get it and she'd act like I'd saved the mission. It was probably her sneaky way of making me do math and help her with shopping she didn't like. But it was fun — we got to hunt around like spies, just the two of us, and laugh like idiots as we ran from one store to the other. I can still remember her fake cackle as she held up a terrible tie for Dad.

By the time we get though half the stores in the mall, I never want to shop with two girls again. It's bad enough to have to spend so much time with Aunt Laura, but with Libby wandering around commenting on all the clothes, I feel like a shopping prisoner. She takes my arm when we get to a jeans store and pretends she's my personal shopper. Aunt Laura's acting all buddy-buddy with Libby and trying to make me laugh, which makes me grumpier.

"Jakob?"

"Huh?"

Libby stands beside me looking into my face. "You okay? You've been staring at that T-shirt for ages."

I look around. We're in Max Clothing, a store that's too expensive for Aunt Laura, but she's looking at the jeans and talking to a sales guy.

"I'm fine," I say. I pull the yellow T-shirt off the table in front of me.

"It's not your colour." Libby digs into the pile and pulls out a blue one. "How about this?"

"Whatever."

She holds the T-shirt up to me. "Blue looks good with your eyes."

"You're not my mother. Can't I find my own clothes?" I walk over to a rack of army pants and pretend to look for my size.

"What's going on?" a voice whispers in my ear.

I spin around so fast I knock Libby into a display of sweatshirts. "Don't do that," I snap. "It's creepy."

Libby pats the sweatshirts back into position. "Carmen has a name for people like — "

"Holy crap, *shut up* about Carmen," I mutter.

Her eyes bug out but she doesn't say anything.

I walk past her and duck behind a stack of jackets. On the other side, Aunt Laura's coming toward me with jeans in both arms. I don't have time to see Libby's face, but I can guess what it looks like.

Two pairs of jeans and three T-shirts later, I'm still in the change room.

Aunt Laura throws a pair of army pants over the door. "How about these?"

Outside the change room, she and Libby are talking but I can't hear what they're saying. For all I know, Libby's telling her how weird I'm being, maybe even about me being out in the yard that first night.

I don't bother trying on the cargo pants, just pull on my old jeans and leave the rest of the clothes crumpled in the change room.

"How were they?" Aunt Laura asks. She holds the three T-shirts and pair of jeans we're going to buy.

"No good," I say.

"Libby's been telling me about her drawings. I hear you've done a few yourself, Jakob."

I clench my teeth to stop J from spitting words out.

"He's pretty good," Libby says. "I wish he'd draw more." It sounds like I'm a preschooler she's encouraging.

"I don't know why you're so excited about it," I say, staring at the fake wood counter as the guy puts the clothes in a bag. "I'm a crappy artist and no one cares about it anyway."

"Jakob." Aunt Laura's hand comes down on my shoulder, pulling me around to face her. "What's with the attitude? Libby's trying to be nice. She's your friend."

"Is she?" I can only look at Aunt Laura for a second, but that's enough to see the laser beams of disapproval she's shooting at me. "Jakob Nebedy, you better start talking. What's going on?" She pulls me out of the store, makes me sit on one of the slippery black leather chairs in the middle of the mall. The ones that are arranged with a rug between them to make you feel like you're in someone's living room. But we're not. We're in the plastic, fake-smelling mall in the middle of the summer. I want to be anywhere but here. I want to be nowhere.

"You've been acting strange for days, and with Mrs. Lester seeing you out at night and your dirty clothes in the washer — what's the deal? Are you into drugs? Talk to me."

"No," I mutter. The rug is red and purple checkers, with gold around each square.

"No to what, Jakob? Explain."

J barges in — he shoves me aside and takes control of my brain. "*I* need to talk? What about you? Why are you talking to *me* about holding things in?"

"Jakob, I think — "

"You're the biggest liar in the world." I'm yelling and it feels good. People are looking but I don't care.

Aunt Laura's face is white. The lines around her eyes and mouth are deeper than I remember. She looks old. "Jakob, can this wait until we get home?"

"Why? So you won't be embarrassed? So you can hide from this stuff for a little longer?"

Libby stands behind Aunt Laura, her hands over her mouth, looking halfway between scared and fascinated.

"They died, okay? I'm the one who should be the most screwed up. I'm their son. But you act like it doesn't matter."

"Jakob, that's not true — "

"Of course it's true!" I shout. "You didn't want to have all their stuff to deal with — you had your own life. I heard you talking to my mom. You said you didn't want to live with us. Then you moved in and all their stuff disappeared. It's like they never existed in the house."

"Stop it!" She grabs my shoulder and shakes me, but not for long, because I rip out of her grasp and sprint down the mall. Everything becomes a blur, stores moving into each other as I race nowhere — just away.

But the end of the mall is the entrance to Sears, and the glaring lights, too-sweet perfume, cheesy music take me back to last Christmas, my mom laughing beside me, showing me a half-price flower vase we could give Aunt Laura. We're going to have an early Christmas because my parents and I are going on vacation and Aunt Laura's alone this year. She's coming over to our house for dinner. I'm stoked to tell her about our holiday plans.

"Jakob. Jakob, listen to me."

Someone's shaking me, moving my body back and forth. It's Aunt Laura, crouching, her arms around me — I can smell her deodorant. We're on the floor beside a round rack of men's pants. I can't figure out if I'm the one who started rocking or if she's moving us both.

"Jakob, I'm sorry. We'll talk about it. I promise. Just don't run."

I stare at the shiny silver arm of the pants rack. Focusing on something calms me down. "I was here with Mom," I hear myself say. "We were buying you that vase for Christmas."

Aunt Laura nods — her chin moves up and down on my head. She breathes deeply and exhales. "The one on the mantelpiece. It's my favourite."

CHAPTER 9

When we get home I go to the bathroom to wash my face. A few tears leaked out on the drive back and I don't like the crusty feeling on my cheeks. Libby has disappeared. I guess it wasn't hard to do when Aunt Laura and I were so distracted.

As I sit on the side of the bath, looking at the blue floor tiles, I hear music come on downstairs. Some terrible girl-band. I've never thought about her music before. For an artist, someone with alternative written all over her, she has pretty boring taste in music. I wonder if she'd like the Cosmic Turkeys.

"Jakob? You okay in there?" Aunt Laura stands outside the door, probably worried I'll get into her razors or something.

"Just a minute," I say. I listen to the muffled music until the song ends and another one starts, sounding exactly the same. I'd rather be downstairs, hanging out with Libby, than about to face Aunt Laura. I could say all kinds of things to Libby and she'd understand. Or she would have before I bit her head off.

"Jakob?"

I get up and open the door.

The photo album Aunt Laura hands me is black and ordinary, but it's stuffed full of photos and papers, as if someone wanted to keep everything but didn't have time to organize it.

I open to the first page. It's me as a baby: four faded photos with captions in my mom's handwriting. *Jakob, six months. Jakob at Brunswick Beach, fourteen months.* The next page is them — my mom and dad at their wedding, on vacation, at someone's house. My dad with a beard and without. I have a vague memory of seeing some of these photos before, but some are brand new to me. It's like looking at their life as if I'm a stranger.

I have a sudden flash of his smile, his white teeth, the rest in shadow. He's in the driver's seat and we're going somewhere. He looks back at me. Headlights of other cars flash in the dark.

"Do you remember the first week?"

I shake my head. The time after the accident is a blur because I was in the hospital with a head injury, then at home in bed most of the time.

"Well, the first week, I was still feeling numb," Aunt Laura says, "so I just did whatever they told me. They said to talk about it with you, even though you weren't always conscious. I talked about Melissa and Charlie — " She squeezes her eyes shut. " — because I thought it might help you to get better faster. I talked about times when you were little and things I'd done with your mom. And even though it made me feel more and more sad, I thought I was helping you — "

I stare at the corner of the album because I can't look at her. This kind of crying might be contagious.

"And then you woke up and I had to tell you all over

again because you'd forgotten. And you just lost it. I thought it might have been easier to hear all those things, but it wasn't. I broke your heart and you broke mine — your little bandaged face." She rubs her eyes. "I couldn't bear it."

"So you stopped talking about it." I stare at a photo of my dad and me and a big cake that says *Happy Birthday, Mom.*

"It was easier because you weren't talking about it either. You didn't speak for weeks, and then when you went back to school, suddenly it was like nothing had happened. You were hanging out with Grant and doing homework and I didn't know what to think."

I didn't know what to think, either. I felt zoned out and separate from everyone, but eventually I got used to it. It was easier not to think about it.

"Your mom made that album for me when you were a baby. I added more as I went through their stuff." She takes a tissue from her pocket. "It was all in the garage until last week. All their things. I couldn't face going through it — like burying them a second time."

"But you went through their stuff?"

She nods. "I found that, started putting more photos in it. My therapist's suggestion."

I flip another page. More parents smiling. Me smiling. One of Aunt Laura holding my hand as I walk on a log at the beach.

"Can I look in the garage?"

"Of course. I think you need to," she says.

"Will you come with me?"

"Are you sure?"

I think for a second. "Yeah."

She smiles a little, leans forward. "Can we have no more secrets or unspoken things? Can we move forward from here with a clean slate?"

Her eyes are so hopeful that I can only nod, while inside J's telling me to keep my mouth shut. I might not be done with roaming, with the memories hidden at the intersection, but this is it — the chance to come clean about everything. I open my mouth.

But just one more night. No one else can do it but me. I promise I'll never lie again after I know the truth.

She's still looking at me, waiting.

"Okay," I say. "Clean slate."

I start at one end of the garage, opening and emptying books and papers and clothes onto the floor. I find my mom's Master's textbooks. My dad's accounting files. A box of baby clothes and toys that must be mine. I can't believe their whole lives fit in these boxes.

"You shouldn't rummage on an empty stomach." Aunt Laura stands in the doorway with a sandwich on a plate. "Need any help?"

I hold up a framed photo of my parents in front of a cheesy painted backdrop.

"Very 1998." Aunt Laura puts the sandwich on a chair and opens another box. "Cookbooks. Melissa was a terrible cook."

"Her lasagna was always burned. I used to think it was supposed to be like that." I pull out a glass bowl that used to sit on the coffee table. I broke it when I was five and Mom glued it back together. The glue has changed colour and you can really see the crack.

"Do you dream about them?" Aunt Laura's thumbing through Christmas cards.

I look down at my hands.

She takes out a stack of CDs. "I do."

I go back to my box, find a bunch of brochures about the Okanagan at the bottom. We went there one summer. Dad went crazy about the stars he could see.

"Do you know where the telescope is?" I ask.

"Huh?" Aunt Laura's got her head in a box.

"My dad's telescope."

"I think it's over there in that big chest." She points to the corner with an armchair, an old lamp and a big wooden chest that used to be in my parents' bedroom.

My heart starts thudding as I walk over and open the lid. I don't know why it makes me nervous. A purple blanket lies on top. I pull it back and underneath is the body of the telescope. I remember when it seemed as big as I was. It's heavy too — there are a lot of mirrors in there to get the magnification. Dad wouldn't let anyone else move it. I brace myself and lift it out.

"It's a monster," Aunt Laura says. She helps me put the body on the blanket.

I reach for the legs. "Did you ever look through it?"

"Once. I think it was the moon. There must be books about stars around here. I thought I saw a star chart or something."

"I have that," I say. "I mean, I found it a while ago."

She looks at me for a long time and I start to feel squirmy.

"This is good, Jakob," she says. "I'm glad we're doing this. It's healthy."

"Yeah," I say, letting out my breath. "Me too."

CHAPTER 10

Soleil's voice echoes in the kitchen, in my head, as I wake up. It's after nine. Why isn't she at work? And why is she in our kitchen?

"Hey, there he is," Soleil exclaims as I wander to the bathroom. "Want to do something fun today, Jakob?"

"Depends what it is," I mumble.

"How about you come with Patrick, Libby and me to Playland?"

Aunt Laura looks at me while I think about it. She knows Dr. Tang told me to stay away from things that might cause me extra stress or anxiety, like racing cars or fast amusement park rides.

Playland used to be the best part of the summer.

"Aren't you supposed to be working?" I ask Soleil.

She leans against the kitchen counter. "My new job doesn't start until tomorrow. Patrick had an appointment this morning so he took the afternoon off too. We'll have you back before dinnertime."

"You're leaving right now?" I ask.

"Well, after you've dressed and eaten something." Soleil laughs. "Libby asked if you could come and I thought it was a great idea. Patrick really wants to meet you."

Right. Patrick. Great.

I take a step into the bathroom. "I don't know if I'm up to it."

Aunt Laura looks like she's trying to diagnose me. "I'm sure you're still worn out from yesterday, but I think it'll be good for you to get out."

"I heard you had a hard day," Soleil says with a smile. I wonder if she can say anything seriously.

"Did Libby tell you?"

She shrugs. "She said you didn't like shopping with girls."

"That's about it," Aunt Laura says, looking at me.

"Please come with us, J-man," Soleil says. "How long's it been since you went to Playland?"

"Last summer, with my parents."

Aunt Laura's still looking at me.

My dad and I did the Gravitator and went in the haunted house three times. Mom actually braved the giant swing even though she was afraid of heights. We all agreed the hot dogs were average but the mini doughnuts were the best in the world. The problem is it won't be the same Playland without them. But then I guess nothing's the same anymore. I can almost hear Aunt Laura in my head: *It's time to start living and moving on.*

They're both waiting. "Okay," I say, "but I need a few minutes."

"Great, J-man," Soleil bounces toward the door. "We'll be waiting downstairs."

After she's gone and I've closed the bathroom door, I hear Aunt Laura walk down the hall. As soon as I've finished peeing, she knocks.

"You know you don't have to go on any rides, right? If it scares you? You can always call me if it gets too overwhelming. I'll be running errands but I'll have my phone."

"It's fine. I'm fine." I keep my hand on the shower tap, waiting until she's gone.

Just as I'm about to turn it on, she says, "Jakob, I think this is really brave of you. I'm glad you're going with them."

"Why?" I ask, although I know what she's going to say.

"You're facing things, getting on with your life. We both need to do that."

I turn on the hot water and let it steam up the room. It's already warm in here, but I like the feeling of the steam surrounding me, sticking to my skin. Making me sweat.

When I come down the back steps, Libby's on the grass with her sketchpad and a piece of charcoal. Looking over her shoulder, I can make out a shaded shape on the paper, maybe a bed or square blanket. At the bottom, two feet stick out.

"Oh, hi," she says distractedly.

"Hey, about yesterday . . ."

"It's no big deal. You've got a lot on your mind. I get it." She looks up and smiles.

"You do?"

"Laura said you didn't mean it. You didn't, did you?"

"No."

"Good."

I feel relieved and worried that she's not making this harder for me. "Well, I do like your drawings. This one looks interesting."

She pulls down the back of her black T-shirt and leans over the drawing. Her nose is an inch from the page, her hair hiding whatever detail she's adding. "By the way, 'interesting' means nothing these days. Carmen says — " She looks up at me for a moment but then keeps going. "Carmen says when people say something you make is interesting, they're using it as a filler word because they can't commit to anything else."

"Oh. Sorry." I step to the side and try to see what she's doing.

She shields the paper.

"How can I say anything else when you won't let me see it?"

"I'm adding something. Give me a second." She leans back and lifts up the sketchbook. "Tell me what you see."

It's still a square blanket or something. The feet still stick out the bottom — bare feet with big toes. But she's added things at the top, shapes at the top of the square. Clothes. A pair of pants and something that could be a shirt. It's not a bed or a blanket. It's a door. The door of a change room.

"Hey there," a man's voice says behind me. "You must be Jakob."

I turn. A tall, lanky guy with long brown hair stands in the doorway of the suite. His face is tanned and his eyes are blue and smiling. J knows it's going to be hard to hate this guy.

"I'm Patrick," he says, coming up the steps and holding out his hand.

It's large and warm and I feel about two feet tall next to him. "I'm Jakob," I say, realizing he already knows this.

"Soleil's told me all about you. I'm glad you're coming along. I'm pretty new to town, so Playland's kind of a big adventure."

"Patrick's from Bella Coola," Libby says behind me.

"You been up north?" Patrick asks me. He stares into my eyes like he's never had a thing to hide, doesn't expect me to either.

"No," I say. I count the weeds growing up under the deck. The only thing I know is there are lots of dogs needing homes up north because they're all strays. The shelters even fly them down sometimes, but the nice-looking ones are off the websites in days.

"Well, it's another world," Patrick says. "The big city kind of freaked me out when I got here. So many people, cars, stuff happening all the time. Everything's so darn fast. Right, Lib?"

"You're right. It is pretty fast," Libby agrees, like they've been buddies for years. It really bugs me and I don't know why.

"Whatcha drawing?" Patrick asks.

Libby shows him the sketchbook. "It's for Jakob."

"Kind of abstract, eh?" Patrick leans in to study the drawing.

"It's me in a change room," I say. "Not really that abstract. She just hasn't drawn the other stuff — walls and floor and people."

"Right. I see that. Kind of like that stuff's not needed because this is the focus."

"Exactly," Libby says excitedly. "It's the story of that moment."

"But there's not really a story there," I say. "I was just trying on clothes."

How come this guy can show up and suddenly start talking about Libby's art like he gets it?

"I wouldn't say that," Patrick says, scratching his neck. His long hair falls in his face and he pulls it back. I never knew a guy with long hair before. "I think it's pretty great," he says. "There's a strong message here. Changing, trying new things, like we do in life. Is that where you're going with it?" He looks at Libby.

Her face is lit up like a Christmas tree. You'd think Patrick was the one to plug the cord into the wall. "Yeah, that's it!"

She so didn't mean that when she drew it. She's just jumping on whatever he says.

"Hey guys. Ready to go?" Soleil closes the door to the suite and locks it. She's wearing a skirt that's a little too short — not that I'm complaining — but you can tell she's trying for her new boyfriend.

"Looking good, babe," Patrick says. "You ready to go, Jakob?"

"Yeah, I guess," I mumble. This is turning out to be a bad idea.

"Libby, can we leave the sketchbook here?" Soleil puts a hand on her hip. "There are too many places to lose it at Playland. You'll be busy, anyway."

"But it's a great place to sketch people."

Soleil gives Libby a no-arguments look. My mom used to give me that too.

"What good's going to Playland if you're just going to be sitting there drawing stuff?" I ask Libby.

Soleil smiles at me as she unlocks the door so Libby can stomp down the steps and put the sketchbook inside.

"Does she draw you a lot?" Patrick asks me.

His voice makes me jump a little. "Uh, no. I mean once or twice. She mostly draws nature and animals."

"She's pretty good. There's something about what she captures that really speaks to you. Don't you think?"

There's that word again: *capture*. It gives me the shivers.

Libby stomps back up the steps, followed by her mom. I'm relieved that I don't have to answer Patrick when Soleil ushers us toward the gate. "Let's get going. Enough messing around. Time to have some serious fun."

It's a little weird to be driving across town with Soleil, Libby and Patrick as if we're a family or something, but after I get used to Soleil's slow driving and Libby's off-key humming to the plastic girl-band song on the radio, it's not so bad.

Patrick assumes I want to go on as many rides as possible and says he'll come with me on the crazier ones if I want, which makes Soleil touch his hand and smile. "Thanks, honey. I get motion sick."

It makes me a little motion sick to watch them.

I haven't decided if I can handle roller coasters or anything, but J keeps whispering that it'll look wimpy to be there looking at all the rides and not go on any, especially if Patrick's going.

"I don't want to go in the haunted house," Libby says. "It'll give me nightmares."

"It's not scary at all," I say. "I went in last year with my dad and we just laughed the whole time." That's not exactly true. We got freaked out in a few places, but we didn't tell my mom that.

Libby looks like she doesn't believe me anyway. "I'd rather not. Being scared doesn't sound like fun to me."

"I'm telling you, it's not scary."

"I guess that's another one for you and me, Jakob," Patrick says.

Soleil gives him another sappy look and it makes me want to puke. I stare out the window at the crappy part of town we're driving through and pretend not to listen to Libby and Patrick's conversation about paint colours. Since Patrick's a house painter, I guess he knows a thing or two.

As soon as we get inside the gates, Libby has to pee. I roll my eyes, then find Patrick smiling at me.

"Girls have small bladders," he says, patting my shoulder

again. “Get used to it. They always gotta pee at the worst times.”

“We’ll meet you by the carousel,” Soleil calls, already following Libby.

Patrick and I wander through the crowd of kids, teenagers, occasional old people and hassled-looking parents. Cotton candy and hot dogs are everywhere — the smell of sugar and ketchup and that delicious, fake meat. My mouth starts to water.

Patrick glances at one of the stands and swears. “Is that what they charge for a hot dog around here? That’s robbery.”

“No, it’s Playland,” I say. “Isn’t it called a captive audience?”

Patrick laughs. “That’s exactly what it is.”

“How about mini doughnuts?” I suggest, thinking since hot dogs seem to be out, maybe I can score some of those. Aunt Laura didn’t give me enough money for a junk food spending spree.

Patrick saunters over to the doughnut stall. He doesn’t walk or stroll. I realize where I’ve seen that before: Chilko saunters too. It’s a loose kind of walking that makes you think they’ve got all the time in the world, but could move fast if they had to.

The doughnuts smell even better than the hot dogs — sweet and cinnamony, golden from the deep fryer. He hands over some money and we rip into the bag.

By the time the girls find us, we have sugar and doughnut remnants all over our hands and faces. “Watch out,” Patrick mutters. “My boyfriend senses are telling me we should have bought them a bag.”

“They can buy their own,” I say. “There’s lots.”

“Ah, young sir, but women always expect you to be the gentleman. Just wait.”

Soleil brushes a spot on Patrick’s face. “Hey, don’t save any for us. We’re fine.”

He looks guilty and smug at the same time. "Jakob here thinks you should get your own. They're not going to run out." He turns to me. "Did I get that right?"

"No way!" I splutter. "I didn't say that. I just meant — "

"It's okay, J-man," Soleil says. "I'm sure it will never happen again." She pokes Patrick in the ribs and they do that nauseating tickley couple thing.

Libby and I take one look at them and walk toward the carousel.

"So you missing your sketchbook yet?" I ask.

"Well, that guy over there would be great to draw." She points to a blue face-painted man on stilts. "But otherwise it's okay." She watches the shiny horses go around the carousel. Kids and parents look out at us as if they're on a stage and we're the audience. Libby smiles up at them and says totally calmly, "By the way, I saw you sneak out the other night."

The glaring carousel music suddenly switches off. The world's sound switches off. I'm alone in the silence that follows her sentence. She watches the people as if nothing has changed.

"What do you mean?" I ask. Hope, hope, hope she's joking.

"I mean, when you snuck out at twelve-fifteen two nights ago, I saw you."

I'm not sure if I should cry or laugh. Thank god someone knows. Make something up, J says. Cover the tracks. "Why didn't you say anything yesterday?" I ask instead.

She looks at me. Her eyes are bluer in the weird light of the carousel. "It wasn't the right time. Was it?"

There's no point in making up a story. Libby's not going to buy it. Or she'll act like she does but I'll know she sees right through it, and me. Just like she does with her drawings.

"Are you in trouble?" she says quietly.

"No." This time it's not really the truth, but I don't know how to explain it to her. In my peripheral, Soleil and Patrick are walking toward us. "Look, just don't say anything. Please. I need to figure some stuff out. I just need time." I hate that I'm bargaining with her. And that she's known for this long.

"You mean you'll go out again?" Libby asks.

Soleil calls to us.

"No. I won't go out again. Just don't say anything. Promise?" I put my hand on her arm, try to make her understand how important this is.

She smiles. "In that case, fine."

"What's fine?" Soleil asks, grabbing Libby from behind and making her shriek.

"Oh, Jakob was asking if I'd give him drawing lessons," she says, grinning like a maniac at me. "And I said I would."

We decide to split up so that Patrick and I can do some rides together while Libby and Soleil can browse the shopping stalls. Why they'd want an overpriced T-shirt covered in sparkles, I have no idea. I'm happy to get away from Libby for a while, but hanging out with Patrick has me kind of nervous too. He seems ready for the craziest rides, while I'm not sure I want to go on any.

"Doom Mountain or Gravitator?" he asks. "Your choice."

Gravitator reminds me of my dad.

"Doom Mountain." I eye the lineup.

"Does it go upside down?"

"No," I say, wondering if he thinks that's good or bad. I don't think I — or even J — could handle going upside down.

Patrick gets in line behind a couple of guys covered in tattoos. "I guess we'll meet our doom, then."

He means it as a joke, but my stomach shudders.

"I think it's great that you're getting along with Libby," he says. "She hasn't had the easiest time. Soleil says she's never had many friends."

The tattooed guys laugh about something and shove each other around. "She's weird, but also kind of cool," I say, and I realize it's truer than I first thought.

He nods. "I'm really impressed with her art. But she's sensitive and that's hard for a kid. Most people probably don't get her."

"How do you know that?" I haven't been able to explain her, but he's right.

Patrick shrugs. "I was like that once. An artsy kid, in my own world. I talked to people who lived in my head. Drove my mother crazy. I had only one friend in high school. He's still my friend, all these years later."

I don't know what to say to that so I just stare at the blobs of dried gum and flattened bits of popcorn on the ground, thinking of something else. "What does the name Chilko mean?'

"Ah, well." Patrick pulls out his wallet. "It's an area, the Chilcotin, near where I grew up. Chilko means *red ochre river.*" He hands me a worn photo of a blue river with a sandy shore under a puffy-cloud sky. A white and black puppy plays in the water. "And Chilko's mom was a red and white husky, so it's kind of an homage to her too. You a dog guy, Jakob?"

My mouth feels dry. "How'd you know?"

He glances at the roller coaster as it swoops down and back up again. "I could have pegged you for one, but George mentioned you might be."

"I've wanted one forever," I say, then wonder if I'm giving something away. "My parents always said next year." I let that hang in the air, not sure how much he knows.

"What about your aunt?"

"Yeah, right. She'll never let me keep a dog in the house."

"Well, you'll just have to hang out with mine," Patrick says. "We're always looking for buddies to walk with. He's actually a pretty fine escape artist. I have to keep him roped because he was getting out of the yard. Huskies are famous for climbing fences."

"I know," I say, feeling the sweat break out on my neck. "I read about it."

He takes a few steps to close the new gap between us and the tattooed guys. "And he got sprayed by a skunk last week. Man, that reeked. No more roaming around for him."

My face feels hot and tight and I pretend to be interested in a couple of girls walking by.

"George said Chilko really took to you," Patrick continues.

"Yeah, I don't know why," I mutter. "He must be really friendly."

Patrick shrugs. "Not with everyone. Huskies are kind of aloof. They're like cats that way. They'll decide to like something or not."

"And they're independent," I say, thinking of how Chilko never really needs me when we're out together.

"Yup. And crazy-strong. Mind of his own when he wants to go somewhere." Patrick looks at me. "I had to interview a few people to find George. I needed someone big, able to handle Chilko's weight and stubbornness."

We're getting close to the front of the line and I'm getting to the end of my rope. J wants to tear into Patrick for not letting me prove myself as a dog walker, for assuming I couldn't do it. I also want to curl up somewhere and block out all the noise. I'm not sure which way is better to fall.

We stand in awkward silence for a minute and I try to think of something to break it. "How long have you had Chilko?" I ask.

"Since he was a pup. You could say he came from a broken home."

"How come?" Something tells me whatever Patrick's going to say will only make this crazy situation harder, but I can't stop myself.

"It's kind of a sad story." Patrick shakes his hair out of his face. "He was the smallest in the litter, if you can believe that. There were four. Three girls and him."

The roller coaster comes back to the station and kids scramble out of it, laughing and shouting.

"His mom was a beauty — pale blue eyes, that reddish fur," Patrick says. "She lived around town, apparently had been someone's at some point, but she'd been a stray for a few years. I'd watched her since the spring, when I first noticed she was pregnant."

"She was just wandering around?"

"That's what strays do. She looked in good shape, though. She was getting food somewhere."

"But how did you know where she'd be?" They're about to load the ride again and suddenly I just want to step out of line. I just want to talk to Patrick about Chilko like we're friends and everything is normal.

"I was painting this house next to a lot that hadn't been built on yet," he says, strolling up as the guy takes our tickets and sends us through the turnstile. "Lots of shrubs and tall grass. Perfect for a dog to have her pups. I looked over one day from the top of my ladder, and there she was, holding one of the pups in her mouth. After I finished work, I went over there and watched her."

We get into the first car of the roller coaster. Patrick's still talking, seems relaxed, but I'm tightening up like a spring. I can't make my hands unclench. Dr. Tang's words of warning fill my head. I try to ignore them by focusing on Patrick's voice.

"She'd made a nest in an old refrigerator box," he's saying. "Pulled in some leaves and rags and made this great den for the pups. I didn't get that close because she was watching me with that mama look, but after I'd been back, brought her food a few times, she let me sit beside her."

A bell rings and the operator comes by to check we're strapped in. Tells us not to put our hands out while the ride is moving. I try to picture Chilko and his mom and sisters — little furballs in an overgrown field, Patrick sitting there watching — but I keep coming back to the present, the bump of the car as people move behind us, shouts from kids waiting in line.

"Well, this is a first for me," Patrick says. "Got to admit I'm a little freaked."

"You are?" I look at him.

His face is pale under his tan. "Yeah, I'm not really great with heights. Or G-forces."

So he hates pretty much everything about these rides. Holy crap. "But you paint houses. Don't you go up ladders?"

The guy pushes a button in the control room and we jerk forward, start moving up the track.

Patrick grips the sides of the seat. "Yeah, but ladders don't go fifty kilometres an hour."

"Great. So neither of us wants to be here," I mutter.

Patrick doesn't hear me.

The car starts to climb. My heart is ramming into my ribs and my palms are sweaty. The strap on my chest feels tight and familiar. I squeeze my eyes shut and try to stay here at Playland, another hot summer day, but suddenly I'm flying back to dark, wet streets — glowing street lights move past the rainy window. We're driving through an intersection. I force my eyes open. The roller coaster thunders and shudders under me. Then we're slipping, the car is spinning in a circle. My neck strains, a yell coming from deep in my throat.

Something squeezes my arm. I flash back to present, where we're riding the track up and up, the loud gears vibrating through me.

Patrick's holding onto my arm. "It's okay, right? How bad can it be?"

As we reach the top of the track, hesitate, I look out over the city, blinking in the bright sun. I can't answer his question.

"We're okay," Patrick says as we start the descent, the people behind us already screaming. "Just remind me not to do this again."

My reply is lost in the roar of the machine.

CHAPTER 11

The light from the street lamp outside the house paints my walls a faint orange. It's 11:00 pm. Aunt Laura went to bed early — headache. There's no TV or music on downstairs. It's a warm night, clouds covering the stars. I won't be able to find Sirius, but at least I know where I'm going now.

After we stumbled off the ride, Patrick and I wandered through the crowds looking for a place to sit down. He looked ready to puke but I was a little distracted. I couldn't get the picture out of my mind.

I see myself standing on the side of the street as our car spins, then tumbles down the bank. I pretend to be a witness. I still can't see what it was that caused the crash. It's the last piece of the puzzle. Maybe when it's complete, I'll stop dreaming about finding it.

Because the floor creaks and Libby might be listening, I slide the stiff frame of my window up as high as it will go. I haven't tried to get out this way since I was nine and playing spies with a kid from across the street. I fell out and sprained my ankle. I'm hoping now I'm tall enough to make the drop.

Before I climb out, I throw the backpack onto the grass, cringing as I wait for a thud. It makes almost no sound. Libby's bedroom window is under Aunt Laura's room, so with any luck she won't hear or see me, even if she's awake.

The walk to Patrick's house — it's hard to call it Chilko's anymore — is fast and slow at the same time. I'm pulled forward by finally knowing what happened the night of the accident, but my gut tells me I'm letting everyone I know down. Including myself.

As I walk along the lane, scouting for lights on in the houses, my skin gets goosebumps. This is the last time. After this, no more lies.

Chilko lies in the middle of the lawn with his head between his paws. I can't see from here if he's asleep or not, but his ears are up, so he knows something's going on. There are no lights on in the house. For a second I wish there were.

"Hey, Chilko," I whisper, putting my nose through the chain-link fence.

He's up instantly, tail wagging. He'd know me anywhere.

We walk the same route as before. I take the lead, making sure to keep us on track so I know exactly where the intersection is.

A few cars pass us, but no one slows down or looks at us. We're invisible tonight. I start to breathe normally. Maybe this is going to work out.

After Ridgeway Avenue we walk past an empty, overgrown lot. Big trees and tall grass fill the space between two houses. My mom always warned me to stay out of places like this. Never know what you might step on.

Chilko heads right into the jungle.

"Hey, come back," I whisper.

He ignores me.

I try to step where the grass has been pressed down into a trail. He disappears behind a round bush. Homeless people live in places like this.

And around the bush I find what I'm afraid of: cardboard boxes and shopping carts and garbage lying around. Someone lives here. Or did. And Chilko's inside their house.

He sniffs inside a big box, every corner, turns around and wags his tail.

"That's someone's house," I whisper. "Let's get out of here, Chilko."

He seems to understand because he takes one more look at the box, then trots past me, back toward the street. I wipe sweat off the back of my neck.

We walk on, in sync with each other, me and my dog. I reach over and rub his ears and he grins at me. I'm connected to him in a way no one else is. I want this feeling to last forever. Somehow everything will be okay.

Chilko stands at the next street corner, sniffing the air. I give him a pat and we cross together.

The problem is, the person I'd like to talk to right now, who'd maybe understand what it feels like to be on my own — who'd probably see some kind of art in being surrounded by silence and the hum of the city — thinks I'm at home in bed. Because I promised her I would be.

I start to get nervous as we come to the corner of Keith and Brooksbank. One block to go. Chilko is happy to wander in front, sniffing bushes and peeing on everything as usual. My spine tingles. It's like waiting for the doctor to give you a shot — you know it's coming, just not when.

The intersection is empty and quiet. On one side, the houses sleep, office buildings dark and deserted. On the other side, the woods that lead down to the river.

I take hold of Chilko's collar as we come to the spot where we stopped last time. My thoughts spin like a dust storm.

Dad's voice is in my ear. *We've been through this a thousand times, Jakob. The answer's still no. Not until you're older.*

Chilko's warm fur keeps me from slipping all the way back. I grip his collar tighter.

"But Dad," I hear myself say. "I can handle the responsibility, I swear."

I'm losing patience with this. Let's talk about something else. Dad's voice is hard and I know I've lost.

"What, like stupid astronomy? That's all you ever want to talk about. Maybe I don't want to go camping next summer."

Dad blinks but says nothing.

Then I see it. In my mind I see myself see it in the road ahead. "Dad, look — there's a dog in the road," I say.

"I'm warning you, don't push me on this, Jakob," Dad growls, looking back at me.

"No, really — "

Mom gasps. Her finger points. "Oh my god, Charlie!" The moment my dad sees it, his mouth opens. His hands jerk the wheel. The flash of something in the headlights, something black. Something furry. It slips out of sight a second before Mom screams. We spin, spin, hit something — a curb — then roll. My mom's ragged voice — *Jakob!* — rips my eardrums and I shake my head back to the present.

I know, finally, as I try to clear my vision, rub my face with my hands. It was a dog. A black dog in the road, and I couldn't warn him in time. He didn't believe me. The screech of tires fills my head, the smell of burning rubber on dry pavement —

But the road was wet when we crashed.

I look up as the sound of Chilko's yelp-scream cuts through the night air.

Where. Where is he? The road. The road is empty. Find him, find that dog. He's my dog. I brought him here.

For a second, two cars pause — one red, one dirty white. Dirty white pulls around red and screeches off. Red stays, door opens.

I fade back to tires and windshield wipers, clicking metal and someone's moan. It's coming from my throat.

Someone's trying to talk to me — they've gotten out of their car and they're looking into my face. It's an old man. He says things that fall apart as soon as they leave his mouth. I try to focus. It feels important.

The old man points to a spot in front of his car. I finally hear him say, "That other car clipped him. Did you see? The car took off and your dog ran into the woods." He points down the road at the tail lights getting smaller and smaller.

"Clipped him?"

"Yeah, caught him on the side. He didn't go under. Damn stupid kids don't stop for anything. I didn't get their licence plate, did you?"

I shake my head.

"Are you okay, son? Your dog was hobbling, but going at some speed. I'm no vet, but that might be a good sign." The man looks hopefully at me, then at the woods.

Dogs run from pain.

They hide somewhere because they feel safer, even if they're badly injured.

"Should you be out this time of night?" he asks. "Are your parents around?"

"They're — " I start to say it, but realize it will only make things worse. "I've got to find him." I start to back away, my mind already listing all the horrible injuries Chilko could have.

"I'll help you look for him." The old man holds up his hand. "I can call animal services."

"No. Please don't call anyone. I have to go," I call, jogging to the edge of the road. But I need help. I need all the help I can get. My throat starts to close as I think of him lying somewhere, dying. It can't be. It can't.

A voice is shouting from far away. I don't know if it's J or me or someone else. *Stupid! Look what happens when you take it too far. This is all your fault.* Now the voice gets more familiar, but the words are harder to take. *This is why we never let you have a dog. This is what happens when you can't be responsible.*

I thrash through small trees and bushes, shining my flashlight, calling Chilko's name. I stop to listen for whining, howling, anything dog-like. Silence.

I gulp air and look around, smelling dirt — the same dirt as that night. Somewhere around here is where our car stopped. Plants have grown up again, hiding the evidence. It couldn't be worse: I'm back where it happened, but for a completely different reason. How could I have been so stupid? "I'm sorry!" I yell. "I'm sorry, I'm sorry!"

Nothing answers me, and I'm not sure who I'm yelling at, but another chunk of sound comes up from somewhere and I yell and yell, burning my throat with how loud it is. Every yell empties me a little more. The trees swallow it up.

Finally I lean on a tree, put my head back and cry.

A branch scratches my cheek. The woods seem to go on forever. I don't even know how far it is until I reach the river. No moon, no stars tonight. In this darkness, I might just end up in the water. Every snap of twig and rustle of leaf could be Chilko, but it's not. He's used to the forest, being alone in it. Huskies are pretty close to wolves as far as dogs go. He could be anywhere.

"Chilko!" I let out the biggest, loudest call I can. It bounces off the trees then disappears. The far-off drone of a car on the road.

I search for what feels like forever, trying to use a system so I don't search around a tree twice, but this is impossible, I realize, as I come to the same short stump. I can't even see any tracks in the dark. My flashlight's getting weaker. My head feels like it weighs fifty kilos.

I'm about to give up, although I still haven't thought about what that means, when my phone rings and makes me jump against a tree. Rubbing my shoulder, I pull the phone out. It could only be Mason. Unless — my mouth goes dry — Aunt Laura discovered I'm not at home.

But it's neither of their numbers. It's Soleil's number. The one taped to the fridge in case I need help when Aunt Laura's not home. But I know it's not Soleil.

I press talk.

"Oh, you are up," Libby says. This seems a little dumb because I'd have to be up to answer the call.

"Yeah, I am," I say, and feel so completely alone that my eyes start prickling again.

"But you're not upstairs."

What's the point in lying now? "No, I'm not."

"What's going on, Jakob? Everyone's worried."

"Who?"

"My mom and your aunt. And me."

"Do they know I'm out?"

"No, but can't you just tell me where you are?"

"I'm in the woods."

"Why?"

"It's a really long story." I push off from the tree, holding the flashlight out until I find a narrow trail that seems to go in the direction of the road.

"Are you in trouble, Jakob? Do you want someone to come and get you?"

God, yes. "God, no," I say. "I'm coming home now."

"But you're going to tell me what's going on. You have to." Her voice is quiet but so sure. It's the most solid thing I have right now.

"Is your mom awake?"

"No. She sleeps like a log. Don't worry. I don't care how long the story is."

Up ahead, I think I can make out the faint light of a street lamp at the top of a bank. I aim for it. "Good," I say, wiping my nose on my sleeve. "Because it'll take me all the way home to tell it."

CHAPTER 12

Somehow it's close to dawn by the time I reach the house. I feel completely empty, like my insides have been scooped out and I'm a walking shell. There's an echo inside me that repeats *my fault, my fault.*

I talked until my tongue got tired and my eyes dried up. The weirdest thing happened — I actually felt lighter. As I told Libby the truth, some of the heaviness left. When I turned the corner onto our street, I almost thought it was gone — that everything would be okay. But then I saw the dark house, remembered that Aunt Laura and Soleil and Patrick didn't know, but that I'd have to tell them, and that Chilko was still missing. The heaviness dropped on me like a piano.

Libby sits on the wall beside the back steps in her yellow pyjamas and a black hoodie. She looks so small but I know that's misleading. There's more there than you think. She smiles as I walk up, the smile of someone who feels happy and sad at the same time.

She holds up a finger. "First, I'll help you look for him, call the pound, whatever you want to do. Second, I won't tell my mom or Patrick — but you have to."

I look at my dirty shoes, her bare feet.

"Third, do you need a hug?"

I start to say no, that's the last thing I need, but she comes at me and I find myself hugging her anyway.

"I think you win the most-in-need-of-human-contact award," she says.

"What?" I ask, stepping back and picking up my bag.

"It's what my mom says when I'm upset. It's pretty stupid, I guess. So what's your plan?"

"We need someone with a car."

"Who?"

I pull out my phone. "My friend Mason."

"Does he know?"

I shake my head, already dialling. It rings, rings and I start to panic. Goes to voicemail.

Libby's looking at me.

"I'll try again," I say. He has to pick up. He has to.

"Why don't you go upstairs, relax, get a drink or something. He's probably just asleep like everyone else in town."

A day ago, Libby's attitude would have made me want to strangle her. But she's right. We agree to meet back here in ten minutes.

In the time it takes me to get a glass of water and change my shirt, which stinks of sweat, only four minutes pass. I can't wait anymore. I sneak back down the steps and hit redial. It rings on and on. I hit redial again. I'm starting to wonder if Mason's phone is at the bottom of a pool when he picks up, fumbling for a second before he says, "Grrph?"

"Mason? Are you up?" I sit down I'm so relieved.

"What the — no. I'm not."

"It's Jakob."

"What freakin' time is it?"

"Uh, early. Look, I know you're tired, but.— "

"More like mostly dead. I'm not a morning person."

I cringe. "But this is such a big emergency I can't even explain everything right now. I just really need your help."

"What — you need money? More skunk shampoo? What else is there?"

"I need you to drive us — me and a friend — to a place."

There's a pause, then muffled groaning. "What is this, some kind of drug handover? Can we talk about this later?"

"No," I say, trying to keep my voice down, but find it rising anyway. "Mason, you helped me out with Chilko before and I need your help again. It's so much more serious this time. Life or death serious."

"This is a lot for my brain right now."

"I just need you to come and pick me up at the corner of West Sixth and Mahon. I'll tell you where to go. I promise I'll never ask you anything like this again. And I'll work your shifts at the store for a year. Or something else — you name it."

"Listen, I don't want to be involved in some drug lord's plans for your dead body."

"I promise there's nothing like that going on. But Chilko might die. Please say you'll come." I want to grovel, but I'm not sure how to do that over the phone.

Mason pauses. "I'm totally going to get into trouble, aren't I?"

I let out my breath. "Me, actually. You'll just be an accomplice."

I have a terrible vision of us sneaking out the gate only to find Aunt Laura or Patrick on the sidewalk waiting for us. They ask us where we're going but we don't say — we just keep walking. They follow, asking us again and again, begging us to say something. Mason's car idles on the corner and we get in, Aunt Laura and Patrick pleading with us through the window. I feel like the smallest speck of dirt.

But as we close the real gate behind us, there's only the empty street and the sun coming up over the far mountains. The clouds have disappeared. Another perfect July day.

"Is that your friend?" Libby asks, pointing down the street as a brown station wagon pulls along the sidewalk.

"How old is he?" Libby asks as Mason gets out.

I'm so relieved it's him, I just start running.

Mason leans against the car. Other than his eyes being half-open, he looks asleep. "You better have a good story."

"Oh, we do," says Libby before I can say anything. "I'm Libby, by the way."

"Hi, Libby?" Mason looks at me with the question on his face.

"Let's get out of here," I say to them both. "I'll explain on the way."

Mason's car smells like roses and candy.

Libby takes one sniff in the back seat and says, "Are you a florist or something?"

Mason gives me a look again, but I haven't had time to explain Libby to him. "My parents own a corner store. They sell flowers."

"It's nice," Libby says, picking up a few rose petals from the floor and dropping them in our laps.

"Okay, so Libby's my neighbour from downstairs," I say. "I thought the more people to search for Chilko, the better."

Mason's eyes fly open. "Wait a minute. Chilko's missing? Didn't you tell your aunt?"

"Yeah, well he's not exactly my dog, remember? He belongs to a guy called Patrick. He's dating Libby's mom."

Mason leans his head on the headrest. "How come every time I see you, things get way complicated?"

Thanks to Mason's crazy-fast driving, we're at the intersection in no time. It's the same and completely different in daylight. For one thing, it's friendlier. You'd never know a dog got hit here last night. Or that two people died in a car accident here six months ago.

"I brought some dog treats," Libby says, already jumping out of the back seat.

We start in the same area I did a few hours ago, but it's a hundred times easier in the day. Things I thought were logs and bushes must have just been shadows — the woods are more open than it seemed last night. Libby goes off in the direction of the river. I'm not sure if we should organize a system, but by the looks of the other two, they're just trying their luck everywhere. We call Chilko's name, three voices in different pitches saying it over and over. The woods seem to swallow it up like it did last night.

I scan under every bush, hoping for a flash of grey fur or white tail. Every so often I think I hear the shout of one of the others, but it always turns out they tripped on a root or walked through a spider's web. An hour passes and all we find are squirrels and candy wrappers.

The sun is up over the trees now and it's getting hot. I pull aside another bunch of branches to peer into a bush.

"How far could he have run, Jakob?" Mason says behind me, sounding exhausted. "I'm pretty sure we've searched every inch of this place."

I throw a stick into the empty bush. "I'm not sure how hurt he is. It was dark. He could have run all the way home for all I know."

"Then we should check there," Libby says from behind me. "Patrick will either be worried sick or at the vet's with him."

I sit on a log that lies across the path. This is what I was hoping wouldn't happen. If there was a chance we could find him this morning, by ourselves, at least when I took him back to Patrick, it would have been me that found him. Now I have to show up empty-handed and tell him everything. Who knows what he'll say. Or do.

Mason pats my shoulder.

"What?" I mutter.

"You sure love that dog, I guess." He sits on the log beside me. "I know you're going to get a whipping, but at least you're doing this because you care. Right?"

"Whatever. Thanks."

"Let's go home," Libby says. "There's nothing else to do."

I put my head in my hands. "This is so messed up."

"Hey, man. This is one of those times."

"What times?"

Mason winks at Libby. She blushes. "A time you're glad you only have to live through once. Like when I dropped a jar of molasses on my foot. Terrible."

I get up. "Mason, he could be dead right now. It's not funny."

"I know it's not funny, Jakob. That's when humour is good. Don't you think so, Libby?"

Libby looks like she can't decide whose side to take.

"Listen, my grandpa died last year and his last request was that everyone at his funeral tell one joke. Preferably about him." Mason shrugs and starts walking down the trail toward the road. "I'm just saying. As the one who was rudely woken up at five in the morning, that's my advice. Now are we going back or what?"

"Let's go, Jakob," Libby says beside me. "Maybe it won't be that bad."

I look around me, wondering if I can make a home for myself in the woods. Just live here for the rest of my life and survive on bugs and leaves. Being a hermit might make up for everything.

I let her go ahead. She walks fast and soon disappears around the curve. I know I should be hurrying — Chilko's still injured somewhere. I only wish I knew where. I take all the air I can into my lungs and let out the loudest, longest shout I can. "Chilko!"

Birds sing back. Nothing else.

CHAPTER 13

"And where have you been?" Aunt Laura says as we walk through the gate. She's standing, arms crossed, on the deck. Waiting.

Libby touches my arm. "Good luck."

"Thanks a lot," I mutter, wishing she wouldn't leave me, but this isn't her mess. It's mine.

I drop onto the couch and wish I could sleep for five days before I have to tell her the truth. I've never been so tired in my life, even after all the other nights roaming.

"What's going on, Jakob? I thought we were being straight with each other." Aunt Laura sits opposite me, trying to look calm, but failing.

"I'm sorry."

"What does that mean? What aren't you telling me?"

"It's nothing illegal," I say.

"Well, thank god for that," she rolls her eyes, then stops. She leans in closer and takes a breath. "Is it about your parents?"

I've forgotten about that part. It was about the accident, only now it's about so much more. I nod. "I went to find the intersection where the accident happened."

Aunt Laura's mouth hangs open.

"I kept having these flashes of the car and Mom and

Dad, but I couldn't remember enough. I went looking for the spot and I found it. Somehow it triggered the memories. I saw it all."

"My god. Why?"

I tell her about the dreams, the pieces that wouldn't fit together.

She shakes her head. "I could have taken you. You should have said something."

"But I've been having the dreams for months and I couldn't tell you," I say. "I needed to go back there one more time to know for sure. A dog was in the road and Dad swerved and we spun around. It wasn't his fault."

"Did you think it was?"

"I didn't know, but now I do. It was mine."

Aunt Laura stares at me. "It was an accident, Jakob. You didn't cause it."

"I did. I kept bugging him about getting a dog and then there was one in the road and he didn't believe me — I tried to warn him — and he almost hit it. We spun out on the wet road. If I hadn't been distracting him, we would have been fine."

She shakes her head but I can see her trying to process what I've said. "No. That's not true. It was a terrible coincidence, but you didn't cause the crash."

"How can you know that?"

"I know because you just told me what happened. It was dark and the road was slippery. A dog ran in front of the car. It was not your fault, Jakob."

"You're wrong. You weren't there. I know what happened now."

Aunt Laura looks at her hands, then at me. She looks for what feels like a whole minute, as if she's seeing me for the first time. "Okay," she says. "Maybe what you say is true."

"It is," I say, feeling the weight of it all over my body.

"It doesn't matter."

I blink fast. "Of course it matters."

"No, it doesn't. Your parents died in a terrible car crash, and you survived. You've been struggling, as I have, to deal with it since it happened. How or why it happened stopped mattering a long time ago." She leans forward and grabs both my knees. "They would forgive you, Jakob. They would forgive you in a second."

I haven't cried this much since I was a kid and road-rashed the whole side of my body falling off my bike. I want to believe her but there's the whole other part of this mess that she still doesn't know about. How can I deserve to live when Chilko's maybe dead somewhere because of me? I let her hug me. I hug her back.

We're just sitting back, wiping our faces when there's a knock at the back door. Soleil peers through the window.

"Sorry to bug you," she says when she's cracked the door. "Patrick's here. He wants to know if you've seen his dog."

I look at the floor but I can feel Aunt Laura's eyes on me.

"Libby said I should come and ask you," Soleil says. "Have you even met Chilko yet, Jakob?"

I take a deep breath, hoping it will slow my heart down. "Yeah, I have. I guess he should come up." I can't look at her — at either of them. Want to run away so their eyes don't bore into me anymore. Soleil disappears silently.

"Jakob, what's going on?" Aunt Laura's hand reaches for me, touches my shoulder.

Steps on the stairs, across the deck, his shadow in the doorway. Then his deep voice: "Morning. Sorry to bother you, but have you seen Chilko? He's missing and I've checked everywhere around my house."

"Jakob?" Aunt Laura's voice is tight.

I glance at Patrick. He looks almost as tired as I feel. His eyes are hollow, missing something that was there the last time I saw him.

And I did that.

"You'd better come in," I say. I don't know how long my voice will hold out before it cracks.

When Patrick's sitting on the couch beside Aunt Laura, I sink back into my spot and grasp at the best way to start. There's no J putting smart words into my mouth. Just me.

They sit across from me, waiting, wondering what I can possibly have to say. Wondering how bad it is.

The story spills out fast but it's all there: each night roaming, the time I met Chilko at Patrick's with Libby. The last two nights, when I stole him from the yard. Last night, when I found the truth about the accident and lost Chilko at the same time. I don't feel anything — not fear or guilt or sadness. Just empty. The emptiest person on the planet. This is what it feels like to steal, to take someone's life or someone they love's life, and be responsible for it.

I can't bear to look up. I don't even know how to apologize for it, so I just say, "I understand if you never forgive me. I don't deserve it." And I realize it's true. I don't deserve to be forgiven by Patrick, but especially not by Chilko, if he's even alive.

"Oh, Jakob." Aunt Laura gets up. "I had no idea. I'm so sorry, Patrick."

I grip the arm of the couch, waiting for him to speak. Nothing is worse than waiting. When I glance up, he's looking at me straight. His eyes are serious, heavy. I can't tell what's behind them. "So you searched the area where the accident happened?"

"Twice. He must have run off. Maybe tried to make his way home." My throat is dry.

"Did you call anyone? Animal shelter or the pound?"

"No." It sounds so stupid that we left it up to ourselves. What was I thinking?

Patrick gets up.

"I'm sorry," I say.

"Me too," he says.

"I'm a terrible person and I should never have done any of it. All I want is for him to be okay."

He starts for the door.

"Jakob, we're going to have to talk about this," Aunt Laura says. "This is a serious issue."

"I'm grounded for life. I ground myself."

"Well, that's not the point — " she begins.

Patrick closes the door behind him without saying goodbye.

"I just don't know what to say," Aunt Laura whispers. "How could you do this?"

I rest my forehead on my knees. I don't know.

The door opens again.

"Before he's grounded for life, Laura — " Patrick pauses just long enough to look me in the eye. "Can he come with me?"

CHAPTER 14

Patrick's truck is old and beat-up, with a really long gearshift and bouncy seats that don't have headrests. A few postcards are fastened to the roof: Tweedsmuir Park and Chilko Lake. I remember the photo of puppy-Chilko playing in the river. Country music plays loud on the radio and Patrick doesn't turn it down. He pulls onto Keith Road then asks me to direct him.

"It's at Keith and Lynnmouth," I say. "We took Seventh until Cygnet Street and then turned onto Keith. Chilko knew the route."

Patrick rubs the bridge of his nose. "You had some secret life. Both of you."

I lean my head against the window as the twangy music plays. Maybe this was a bad idea.

We're almost there when he turns off the radio and turns to me. "I never finished telling you about when I got Chilko." He pauses to see if I'm listening.

"You don't have to," I say. "It's way too hard now."

"For you or me?"

I cringe as I look over at him. "I don't want to make you feel worse."

"Hard to do that at this point."

I hide my face with my hands. "Oh god. I'm *sorry.*"

"No, that's not what I mean. I'm just saying I might as well talk about it. Who knows — maybe it'll feel better." Suddenly he pulls the truck over. "We're here."

I can't believe how well I know this intersection now. I've been here three times in the past twenty-four hours.

Patrick gets out of the truck with Chilko's leash in his hand. I force myself to follow.

"I told you Chilko's mom had this great den in the empty lot, right?" We take the path down into the woods. The same path I've seen in pitch black, dawn and daytime. "She was letting me hang out with them, even play with the pups." He calls Chilko's name in a loud, low voice. No answer. He turns to look into a cleared area, calling again.

"If you knew she was a stray, why didn't you take her home?" I ask.

"Didn't seem to be a point. She was happy, healthy. The pups were doing fine. I saw them every day. I figured when they were old enough I'd call a vet, get them vaccinated, and they'd adopt them out. And I liked having them to myself."

"But something happened," I say, because I can feel it like a bend in the trail — this story won't end well.

"Yup. The developer of the lot showed up before I got there one morning. He must have called animal control because they were all gone. The box was there, but no mom, no pups. I was pretty angry. With the guy and with myself."

"Why with yourself?" I ask, but I think I know.

"I should have thought about the pups' safety, not just what I was getting from them. They should have gone to a place where they could have been looked after."

"But she was doing fine on her own, you said."

"Yeah, she was. But I forgot that other people don't always

see things that way. And she was squatting on someone's land. Just a matter of time."

"So did you find them?"

"Well, yeah, I did." Patrick looks at me sideways.

"Don't say they killed them."

His eyebrows join together. "Only Mom. She got really angry that they wanted to move the pups. I guess she bit someone pretty badly. They euthanized her."

"No!" I shout. "How could they? Didn't they think about the puppies?"

"I'm not sure they cared."

"So you found the puppies and got Chilko?"

"I didn't know anything about his mom being killed at that point. I was still at the lot, wondering what had happened. Then I saw a black and white thing under a bush."

"Chilko," I say, relief flooding through me. "They forgot him."

"Or missed him," Patrick says. "I reached for him, but he squirmed away. As I went around to try from the other side, he scrambled into the big old box, calling for his mom and sisters. It was the saddest thing I ever saw." He pauses and puts his head back, letting out Chilko's name in a long, low howl.

I can't move. My throat is dry and achy and I want to turn away, but I can't.

And then it hits me. The cardboard box. The empty lot. Why didn't I think of it before? "I think I know where he is." I'm already running.

"Turn left here." My guts squirm as we take the corner onto the street with the hippie houses. The box he was so interested in last night. It has to be. Please, please let him be here.

"There?" Patrick pulls over.

I'm already out of the truck before he's turned off the engine. I don't even look for cars — just sprint across the street yelling his name, heart hammering in my chest.

The box is still there. A corner of it sticks out behind the bush. I yell his name over and over, stepping through the rags and garbage as Patrick comes up behind me.

And inside the box is our dog. Chilko, curled with his head on his back paws. He lets out a whine, only thumps his tail a little, but he's there. He's alive.

He's soft and warm and smelly and alive.

And then I'm seeing it from above, watching myself touch his paw, Patrick lean in to talk to him, check his body over. The Jakob beside them is crying, but from here my face doesn't feel wet. There's a warm weight on my shoulders like a pair of hands. They press me back to the ground. *It's okay, Jakob. It's okay.* And when Patrick turns to me, saying something with an almost-smile, it is. Not perfect or normal or easy. But okay.

Acknowledgements

Realizing the dream of being a writer has taken a lifetime, and there are a lifetime's worth of people to thank. First, my elementary and high school teachers who encouraged writing — and reading. Without reading obsessively as a child, all this never would have happened. Next, the university instructors who guided my studies. I was able to transform my passion into a craft because of those gifted and generous writers.

This story started as a rough draft passed around a small but diligent writing group. It then became a second rough draft, passed around again. Thank you, Kathy Para, Rachelle Delaney, John Mavin, Carolyn Jarvis for your insights and suggestions early on. Kellee Ngan for her astute and excellent comments on a later draft. Also, an amazing network of writer friends who offer support, critical insight and laughter.

Others who have helped in strange and wonderful ways: Christina Mavinic (for help with nurse-speak) Kirsti Ziola (for the you-know-what), Hannah Tunnicliffe (for being fabulous), Théo Fraser Armstrong (for photography and therapeutic coffees).

Vielen Dank to my parents for their love, support and, recently, babysitting services, and my sister for letting me tell her rambling stories on family hikes all those years ago.

Big thanks to my agent, Louise Lamont, and editor, Anne Shone, for their confidence in the story and expert help in polishing.

And last, my husband, Daryl: thank you for being my best friend, champion and assistant plot-knot-untangler. And to our daughter, Elodie, for being adorable and wonderfully oblivious.

About the Author

Ria Voros has known for a long time that she wanted to write a story about a dog. Her own rescue dog, Pender, was partly the inspiration for Chilko. He was a shepherd-husky cross — although everyone thought he was part wolf — and was a constant companion during the writing of *Nobody's Dog*. Ria says, "As the story unfolded, I realized Jakob had a lot to learn from Chilko, not only about dogs, but also about life. I went through the same process with Pender when I adopted him from a shelter. In the end, both Jakob and I are better people because of the relationships we've had with our dogs."

Ria is a graduate of the University of British Columbia's Creative Writing MFA program. She has published fiction and poetry in literary journals and has won several poetry and creative writing prizes. She has also taught courses in fiction, poetry, literature and writing for children. *Nobody's Dog* is her first novel. Ria lives in Nanaimo, British Columbia, with her family.

About the Author

[illegible]

[illegible]